Beneath the Surface

By: PAULA AIRD

© Copyright 2006 Paula Aird.
All rights reserved. No part of this publication may be reproduced, stored in a retrieval system, or transmitted, in any form or by any means, electronic, mechanical, photocopying, recording, or otherwise, without the written prior permission of the author.

This is a work of fiction. Names, characters - with the exception of well-known public figures, many locations, organizations and incidents are a product of the author's imagination or are used fictitiously. Any resemblance to actual events, locales, organizations or persons living or dead is entirely coincidental.

Beneath the Surface: a novel
Authors Canadian (English) Caribbean fiction
Grenada - fiction
Ontario - fiction
Women - Black - fiction

Note for Librarians: A cataloguing record for this book is available from Library and Archives Canada at www.collectionscanada.ca/amicus/index-e.html
ISBN 1-4120-8943-3

Printed in Victoria, BC, Canada. Printed on paper with minimum 30% recycled fibre.
Trafford's print shop runs on "green energy" from solar, wind and other environmentally-friendly power sources.

TRAFFORD
PUBLISHING

Offices in Canada, USA, Ireland and UK

Book sales for North America and international:
Trafford Publishing, 6E–2333 Government St.,
Victoria, BC V8T 4P4 CANADA
phone 250 383 6864 (toll-free 1 888 232 4444)
fax 250 383 6804; email to orders@trafford.com

Book sales in Europe:
Trafford Publishing (UK) Limited, 9 Park End Street, 2nd Floor
Oxford, UK OX1 1HH UNITED KINGDOM
phone 44 (0)1865 722 113 (local rate 0845 230 9601)
facsimile 44 (0)1865 722 868; info.uk@trafford.com

Order online at:
trafford.com/06-0699

10 9 8 7 6 5 4 3 2

DEDICATION

This novel is dedicated to my family and relatives. Upon whichever branch of the Grant—Benjamin—Aird —Langaigne family trees you may abide, or be attached to, may the resplendence of the sun envelop you, permitting an abundance of those heavenly blossoms - peace, joy and happiness.

ACKNOWLEDGEMENTS

To my sister Joan Stephens, who was my first editor. My heartfelt thanks for reading and editing this manuscript and giving me your candid and uplifting comments as well as your support.

I was honoured to have the author Cassandra Darden Bell read this manuscript and provide me such positive comments. Please accept my sincere thanks Cassandra.

My friend Dawn Brown - an author herself. I am grateful Dawn for your useful critiques and encouragement as well as generous offers of assistance, not the least of which was engaging the services of the very skilled Dr. Gail Johnson, who did an excellent job at editing and provided me with many useful suggestions. Thanks a million, Gail.

Many thanks are due to my dear mother-in-law Ursula Aird, for allowing me to use her as a 'sounding board' when I gave her my manuscript to read. Mum, I deeply appreciate your encouraging remarks and support.

It was my great pleasure to meet Dr. June Marion James during a visit to Winnipeg. Sincere thanks June for taking time from your busy schedule to read the manuscript and providing me such uplifting comments.

I am grateful to the ladies of the CLC for discussing my novel - *What Goes Around...* at their book club. They tell it like it is and continue to be a source of sustenance and inspiration to me.

I cannot sufficiently thank all those family members, friends and acquaintances, many of whom contacted me after reading my debut novel and gave me such terrific feedback. You literally spread the word for me. Some of you have let me know that you are anxiously awaiting this my second novel. You are a great reservoir of strength and encouragement for which I am truly appreciative.

Special thanks to Keith – my final editor – for his superb editing skills. However, while your critiques and insightful comments are important to me, invaluable are your support and encouragement.

Finally I thank the Creator for making all of the above possible.

Beneath the Surface

PREFACE

After reading *What Goes Around...* many readers commented on how accurately it portrayed their own stories. Many requested a sequel. What happened to Joshua and Jolene, they wanted to know. One reader remarked that the story of first generation children of immigrant parents from the Caribbean is seldom told and urged that a sequel be done embodying this theme.

So I have put pen to paper again, not necessarily in response to these requests, I must confess, but simply because it gives me great pleasure to do so. *Beneath the Surface* tells the story of yet another section of the Caribbean diaspora, through the medium of fiction. Several characters from *What Goes Around...* play minor roles in this story or are mentioned in passing.

Most of the story takes place in Ottawa, Canada, where Boni Burke, the protagonist, has been living for more than fifteen years. She was born in the Caribbean island of Grenada and through her we are allowed a peak at the day-to-day lives of Grenadians – their struggles and their triumphs.

The novel touches on the lives of many West Indians who leave their homelands in search of better educational or economic opportunities. The complexity of relationships is observed. How do the children, especially those born in the new country fare? Do they maintain any links with the homelands of their parents? *Beneath the Surface* looks at a small sliver of the diversity of experiences that exists.

1

"Hey... what the...?" my friend Regina blurted out as she suddenly compressed the break pedal of her car. It was a clear and beautiful summer day as we traveled west on highway 7 *en route* to a baseball game in Toronto. I looked up from the magazine I was thumbing through to see the occupants of the car ahead signaling wildly at us as they too reduced their speed. Then we saw it. A car driving in the opposite direction was slowly crossing over the median and was heading across two lanes of oncoming traffic into our path.

"But there's no one driving," I exclaimed as the car passed very slowly in front of us, missing us by a hair. Then I noticed that the driver was convulsing. She seemed to be having an epileptic fit. The car slowly crossed over two lanes and shoulder and finally settled down in the ditch to our right. Regina and I along with several other motorists and passengers stopped and went to the woman's assistance. With her was a little boy who looked about five or six years old.

The woman came to and seemed stunned. She was deathly pale. Saliva was trickling down her chin. She seemed in her mid to late thirties.

"Mum" her little boy said. "We're in the ditch."

"Oh no...we're not," she responded while nervously looking around her. "Shoot" she said frowning, realizing with surprise that they were indeed in a ditch.

"You need to go to the hospital," one middle aged woman peering through the car window suggested to her. "And how you're doing little fellow?" she asked the little boy who seemed quite bright and curious. Perhaps he saw this as an interesting sort of game.

"I'm okay now," the woman in the ditch insisted. "I'll be on my way as soon as I can get out of here."

She seemed very anxious to continue her journey and was alarmed when she learned that someone had called 911.

"No you're not okay," Regina told her gently as she handed her a tissue to wipe the spittle from her face.

"It's dangerous for you to be driving," I added. "You could easily have killed yourself and this little fellow here." That did it. A change came over the woman. Tears welled up in her eyes.

"It's just that I've been having a rough time recently" she admitted in a foreign accent that I couldn't place, as she tried to straighten her bleached, tousled hair. She had full cheeks and on her forehead was a darkened birthmark as if a passing bird had unwittingly crapped on her.

The Police arrived shortly after and took control. Regina and I returned to her car and continued our journey.

"They say misfortune happens in threes," I said to Regina. "I've already had two this week and I don't think I could cope with any more."

Regina shook her head. "Whew! What a narrow escape!" she commented. "I hope that woman gets some help."

"Yeah I hope she does," I answered, then returning the focus to me continued, "I've had my quota."

"Poor Boni" Regina teased, smiling at my imitation African head wrap. "But you should have known better than to let Hurricane Ad mess with your hair."

"I certainly won't get caught again. Once bitten twice shy," I remarked. I loosened the head wrap, which was beginning to make my head feel hot.

Last Saturday misfortune number one had struck. I stupidly allowed Adlyn Mascoll to relax my hair. Adlyn and I worked for *Universal* hospital and over the years we had become friends - sort of. Sometimes I found her much too dictatorial and overbearing. We were having coffee in the cafeteria when I mentioned that I was going to Montreal that Saturday to get my hair done.

"What you havin' done?" she asked me.

"I'm getting it relaxed," I answered.

"Cha man! You don' have fi go all de way in Montreal for dat. Mek me do it for you nuh." When with other Caribbean folk such as myself, Adlyn loved to lapse into her island dialect. I knew that she had quite a lucrative business on the side doing hair. She was excellent at hair braiding. I didn't know about her expertise at hair relaxing but she seemed very confident.

"Yeah man ... come over Saturday morning and me do it for you. Me have a lot of product at home fi use up." That last statement should have pressed my alert button but unfortunately it didn't.

"You sure?" I was warming to the idea of just going over to Ad's home in south Ottawa instead of journeying all the way to my faithful hairdresser on St. Catherine's street in Montreal, to get my hair done.

"Me fix you up real nice" she assured me confidently.

Well she certainly fixed me up. I'm not sure about the 'real nice' part. Either she used too strong a relaxer or she left it in too long. My scalp began to tingle then burn after a few minutes so I called out to Ad who was chatting on the phone. She signaled to me that the call was long distance but she was coming right away.

It seemed like an eternity before she actually got to me.

"Dat was Sharon," she said, as if I cared two hoots.

"Quick...get this relaxer out me hair fast" I answered loudly, ignoring reference to her stepdaughter Sharon who was always full of drama.

When she tried to rinse out the relaxer from my burning scalp, my hair simply eased its way into the sink. It was history. I was furious.

"What you done to me hair?" I asked angrily as I looked from the bathroom sink to the mirror. "Oh my gosh!" I said as the full scope of what happened hit me. Ad was visibly shaken but would she apologize and eat some humble pie for a change? Oh no! Not Adlyn Mascoll.

"Why you never tell me you have tender scalp?" she accused me, as if this whole fiasco was my fault.

"There's nothing wrong with my damn scalp" I screamed. This was adding insult to injury. The strands of hair still on my head easily surrendered to my touch.

"Never mind…it soon grow back," she purred softly while coming towards me with a pair of scissors. "Mek me shape it out for you nuh."

"Don' touch me hair," I replied angrily as hot tears rushed down my cheeks. How the hell was I going to go to work with this mess on my head now, I wondered. Thankfully I recalled that I was off work for part of the following week. But I was hoping to make an impression on a guy Regina was hooking me up with. This couldn't have happened at a worse time. I grabbed my purse and denim jacket and stormed out of Ad's house, slamming the door loudly behind me. Luckily in my purse I found a scarf, which I just tied around my head as I waited at the bus stop.

That was two days ago. Now today Regina and I almost got swiped by that poor woman's car. I felt sorry for her, whoever she was, and hoped she was able to straighten out herself. When compared with real problems out there, hair didn't seem that important. I hadn't seen Ad since the horrible hair incident but she did send over her husband, Erbie, with some curry goat and rice 'n peas for me the following day. It was delicious. I guess that was Ad's way of apologizing. I called her work number and was relieved when she wasn't there. I left a voice mail message telling her thanks. I wasn't ready to speak directly to her yet.

"Do you want us to stop off at the Scarborough town centre before we check into the hotel?" Regina wanted to know.

"Why...what for?"

Regina frowned at me. "For the wig nuh." She had suggested I buy myself a nice, short, wig at the town centre. She knew a place, she said, where the fit and quality were so good, one would swear the hair was the wearer's own and the price wasn't bad either.

"I don't know," I said. As far as I was concerned a wig is a wig is a wig. Those things always shout 'Falsie!' at me.

"Well you don't want Todd to see your head looking like this," she said to me. Todd was her friend Veronique's cousin that she was attempting to hook me up with. He and Veronique, had both lived briefly in London, England before coming to Canada. I felt like saying that Todd's head was probably in worse shape than mine. Sometimes I wondered why instead of putting so much energy into hooking me up, Regina didn't try to hook up herself. Besides, I didn't feel like wasting any more money. If Regina and I were together no fellow that wasn't blind would choose me over her. Many found her gorgeous figure and honey-coloured skin irresistible and no matter what she did with her hair it looked great. The managers of cosmetic and beauty counters at department stores have been known to hire Regina without even viewing her resumé. They knew she would attract customers to her counter. And indeed she did.

I first noticed Regina five years ago at the *Beauty Fire* counter at a department store in Ottawa. I figured anyone looking like she did, should be able to help me choose a lipstick and some eye makeup. The very next Sunday, we unexpectedly bumped into each other at the church I sometimes attend. She was with her cute, little daughter, Tiffany. We were both surprised to see each other. She said she had recently moved to Ottawa from Montreal. We exchanged telephone numbers and gradually became friends. Since we both lived in the same end of the city, I frequently baby-sat Tiffany for her.

However, as my mother always says, all that glitters is not gold. Sitting in my living room one day Regina revealed all about her cheating husband, Michael, to me. She had returned to their home in Montreal unexpectedly one day and busted her husband with their next-door neighbour.

"Were there no signs before?" I asked her.

"Of course there were," she replied. "But I guess I was in deep denial. Until that fateful Friday when I let myself into the apartment and pushed opened the door to the bedroom."

Regina didn't remember too much of that day but she did recall throwing objects around with superhuman strength. When an arm came around her neck she literally took a piece out of it. She remembered Michael sitting on top of her and almost choking her to get her to stop, while the neighbour sought refuge behind a locked bathroom door.

Bruised and hurt, both physically and emotionally, Regina picked up Tiffany from school that afternoon and they both checked into a motel that night. She was not returning to live in that apartment. It was one thing having an affair, but it was a double whammy when the intruder posed as the couple's friend. As far as she was concerned the point of no return had been reached.

Since Michael had signed the lease for the apartment in which they lived, she was not concerned about leaving him to deal with the rent. The next day she moved all her belongings and her daughter's into storage at her friend Veronique's basement. Then she submitted her resignation at work. She couldn't stand living and working in the same city as Michael anymore. She would make a clean break and the sooner the better.

The only problem was Tiffany. She hated having to uproot her poor daughter from both her school and home so suddenly. She definitely was not leaving her with her father. Once again, Veronique who lived a few minutes drive away came to her aid.

Regina packed a suitcase and came to Ottawa the following week. By the next day she had procured for herself a job at a department store cosmetic counter and was to start the following week. Although Veronique had given Regina the name and phone number of her friend Adlyn Mascoll, who could possibly put her up, Regina preferred to live at the Y until she had enough money to pay down for the rental of an apartment for herself and Tiffany. But her heart was filled with sadness and anger.

"People always say I'm lucky ... for having good looks," she said to me that Sunday afternoon.

"Well you are," I replied. "Did I not hear you say how easily you landed your new job at *Beauty Fire*? They didn't even look at your resumé."

"Okay Boni," Regina pouted as we sat around my rickety kitchen table drinking lemonade. "But how far does it get me in the 'Love' department eh?... Not far."

"Well...let's exchange looks then," I chided her. We both knew that it wasn't raining men in my neck of the woods either. But it was much too sunny and beautiful a day to dwell on anything but the positive. I didn't want to argue with Regina but I knew that girl wouldn't want to exchange herself with me for one minute, even if I came with a university degree and, as a nurse, I made a fairly decent salary at the *Universal*.

"So?" Regina nudged my arm, rousing me from my daydreaming. "You want me to take the exit for the town centre?"

"Nah...let's go straight" I replied. "I'm not in the mood for wig shopping today."

2

Regina and I checked into an elegant hotel in downtown Toronto.

"We have a room reserved for Regina Doyle and Boni Burke," squeaked the clerk behind the desk as she checked the reservations and handed two card keys to Regina.

I almost choked when I saw how much the room cost per night. I couldn't believe that Regina. The woman was as poor as a church mouse having a child to raise and all, without any support from her deadbeat ex-husband, but did not mind living high on the hog.

"You must be crazy!" I blurted out as soon as we were some distance from the front desk. Even with splitting the cost in two, it was still a tidy sum.

"Cool it Boni," she said. "It's just for one night. Maybe Todd will be able to put us up for the next night." There went Regina again. She hardly knew this Todd guy – except that he was a cousin of her friend Veronique. She'd met him just once before to my knowledge, but there she went babbling about him being able to put us up. The man could be a Jack the Ripper for all we knew.

"Well whatever...but I'm not staying here another night," I said rather ticked off.
"Okay...okay" said Regina as she shook her head. She was always accusing me of being cheap.
"There's no way I'm going to throw away my hard earned money on some damn hotel room," I told her. I had to admit the room wasn't bad but certainly not as flashy as promised by the lobby with its lavish waterfalls and greenery. I felt gypped. "Do you know that most of the patrons here can probably write off this expense as a tax exemption or have their companies pick up the tab? We're the only two jackasses here."
Regina was not phased. "Come on Boni... let's just live it up for one single night nuh," she said as she shrugged her shoulders.
I decided to cool it after that. I didn't want to be too much of a wet blanket but I was keeping a watchful eye on that Regina to make sure she didn't use anything from the mini-bar in the room. I understood that she had to make long distance calls to Ottawa from time to time to check up on her daughter, Tiffany. But I wasn't about to spend a fortune on overpriced nonsense from the mini-bar.
"At least let's go enjoy the pool and sauna this afternoon ... it's all included," said Regina after we'd enjoyed the fried chicken and ribs I'd packed for lunch. Pool? I hadn't thought out how I was going to use the pool with my patchy hair revealed to the world. How would a head wrap look in the pool? The shaver in the bathroom gave me an idea. With Regina's help, I adjusted the sides and back to just a whisper of hair. Then we shaped the top. With a bit of gel it looked rather nice, I had to admit.

The pool was refreshing and so was the sauna. I felt attractive in my orange and yellow floral swimsuit and short hair. There were several hotel guests at the pool. I have to admit the lack of those thirty pounds I dropped this past year was doing wonders for my self-esteem. Needless to say Regina was as elegant as ever in a simple black suit. That girl would look good in a crocus bag.

Back in our room I slipped into my jeans and Bob Marley tee shirt. "Let's go for a walk," I said to Regina. I knew she was hoping that I would change my mind about checking out of the hotel after one night. But I was on to her. What I meant was 'let's go check out cheaper accommodation' but I didn't want 'to wild' her.

"I'm tired," she said yawning but nevertheless flicking on the TV with the remote. Maybe she was on to me too. Sure, I thought. But I wasn't giving up. I checked the phone book and my Toronto map, then set out from the hotel alone walking towards the subway. There was a little motel two subway stops away that I was going to check out.

I found the motel quite easily. It was in a convenient location with parking. It seemed quite adequate. But above all it cost less than half of what we were currently doling out. There were no vacancies at the time but one room would become vacant the next day. That suited me just fine. Too bad Regina was too tired to come with me, so I had to make the decision all by myself. I gave a deposit to ensure that the room would be reserved for us the next day.

I looked around for some time in the stores and bought myself some huge floppy earrings. There was an energy about this city that one could not deny. I browsed for a while in a bookstore and indulged my habit of people watching. If there ever was a truly multicultural city, this was it.

It was getting dark by the time I headed back to the hotel. On my way I picked up some fast food for Regina and me. Even though I watched my weight, I wasn't one of those 'hung up' people. The odd time I would have some fries or whatever, so long as I didn't make it a habit.

"I brought us some food," I announced cheerfully, pushing the door to our hotel room open with my hip before I realized that Regina had already ordered room service for herself. A tray with used dishes gazed at me from the table near the window.

"I was starved," she said noticing the frown on my face. "And I didn't know how long you were going to be gone."

I felt irritated. Wasn't she the one who pulled me all the way here and now she was hell bent on doing everything on her own. "Oh well," I said as I sat down to my fish burger and fries.

"Smells good."

"And guess what... I found us a room in a motel." I knew that was not what my girl wanted to hear but she forced herself to put on a good face.

"Yes?"

"It's a little motel on the corner of Blew and Hunter" I replied, giving her all the details.

The next day in preparation for the baseball game and also as Regina insisted, to make a good impression on Todd, she did my makeup for me. The floppy earrings

I'd purchased went superbly with my short hair, giving me the sensation of being free. I actually felt beautiful.

Todd was waiting for us in front of the stadium with the promised tickets. We had excellent seats. My first impression of Todd was that he could stand to lose some pounds. I knew exactly why Regina didn't consider him her type. She liked her men good looking and well chiseled like her ex-husband, Michael. Todd was a big, bearded fellow - well over six feet tall, with a booming voice.

It was my first experience in the skydome and I enjoyed the atmosphere there as much as I enjoyed the baseball game itself even though if the truth be known, I didn't have a clue about baseball. But I learned real fast. It was like rounders but not quite and like cricket but not quite. Pretty soon I was clapping and yelling along with Regina, Todd and everyone else. I leaped into the air for the fly ball that came shooting in our direction, just like a real fan.

After the game we went to a seafood restaurant. Todd was hilarious and he didn't mind enjoying a joke at someone else's expense. Right away when he heard my family name was Burke, he started calling me BeeBee. He was tickled at the story of how I came by my name. When I was born my father came into the room and declared "What a cute little bunny face she's got!" That did it. Everyone started calling me Bunnyface or Bunny from then on. At my Baptism, however, the name got changed from Bunnyface to Boniface in honour of the saint. Either name is equally ridiculous to me but I don't mind being called Boni. It sounds like 'pretty'.

Todd wanted to know if we knew a Mascoll fellow in Ottawa, who was married to a nurse. He thought she worked for *Universal*.

"Are you talking about Ad and Erbie?" I asked.

"We have friends called Adlyn and Erbie Mascoll" Regina added.

"This fellow's name is Herbert Mascoll. We used to play cricket together long ago... actually he used to coach our team." Suddenly a light went on in Todd's eyes and looking at us he started to roar with laughter. "You mean y'all been calling de man 'Erbie' all this time?"

"Well that's how his wife calls him," I defended myself and Regina. It was just dawning on me that Erbie's name was actually Herbert. For years I'd been calling him Erbie. But that was Ad's fault. That day I went over to their house to get my hair done I distinctly remember Ad complaining that "Erbie is a pain in the harse!" When she was excited she dropped *Hs* and put them in front of vowels where they didn't belong.

"I wonder how many other names Adlyn have y'all mutilating like this." Todd was determined to poke fun at us.

"Well he answers to what we call him," said Regina giggling.

"Of course he answers. You want his wife to bop him one nuh?" We were all giggling now. Todd continued. "You don' see her size compared to his?" Soaking wet, Herbie had to have been half of Ad's *avoidupois*.

When Regina saw fit to relate to Todd all about my hair escapade with Adlyn, I thought the management was going to evict us from the restaurant - we were laughing so hard.

"But it look real nice though," said Todd finally getting serious. Then he had to get a little jab in. "That no-hair style suit you real good."

After leaving the restaurant, Todd escorted us back to our motel. We walked along Blew street which was busy and festive. I found myself enjoying Toronto. We agreed to meet him the following morning for a late breakfast before we headed back to Ottawa. He was going to come to the motel to get us.

"So? How you like him?" asked Regina poking me in the ribs after he left.

"He's funny..." I answered.

"Yeah..." she said looking as though she'd finally succeeded in making a match. "Both a' y'all funny the same way."

If Regina thought the only dimension to a relationship was a sense of humour, she had a lot to learn about me. She and Adlyn were constantly on a crusade to get me hitched. But I thought they were missing a big fact - that while I wanted a man in my life, and it would certainly be nice to share life with someone, I did not need one. Adlyn herself had seen the potential in a penniless divorcee and hitched on to him. I believed she considered him a work in progress.

"What does he do for a living?" I asked Regina. I realized I didn't know where Todd lived or his occupation.

"I think Veronique said he works in sales."

"Selling what?"

"I'm not sure... why don't you ask him yourself tomorrow?" Regina sounded a little peeved. We were in the room now and I could sense she was comparing this one to the more luxurious one the night before. But I didn't care. This room, with a double bed and a pull-out cot, was adequate. To go easy on Regina, I decided to take the cot and let her have the double bed all to herself. So at least she couldn't complain about being cramped for space.

I flicked on the TV but my eyes were heavy with sleep. I vaguely remembered a reporter talking about the Anita Hill/Clarence Thomas conundrum in the United States that was dominating the news media. I fell asleep on the cot without even pulling it out.

The ringing of the phone awakened me from a deep slumber. Looking at my watch I realized it was after nine o'clock in the morning. Todd was coming at ten. The sound of the shower from the bathroom informed me that Regina was already up and about.

"Hello" I answered as I picked up the receiver.

"Aunt Boni...it's Tiffany...can I speak with Mum please?"

"Hi Tiff...Mum's in the bathroom...but hold on...I'll get her." I was about to ask Tiffany how her Florence Nightingale project, that I had agreed to help her with, was coming along, but something in her voice made me drop that idea quickly.

Regina came out of the bathroom and I heard her talking to her daughter on the phone.

"But Tiff...it's only nine thirty...I'll be home this evening and then we can go to a restaurant... okay?

"Aunt Ad made you pancakes for breakfast? That's good… She didn't have any whipped cream? …only syrup?"

While Regina was talking on the phone I decided to use the bathroom. That little girl of hers was pulling a guilt trip on her mother again. And if you asked me I would say she was eating far too much sugary foods. She wanted whipped cream on her pancakes for breakfast? Puhlease! It's already telling on her - she's fast becoming a little 'fatso'.

I was still in the bathroom when I heard Todd's knock on the room door. Regina let him in and I heard them talking and snickering in the room.

"Hi BeeBee" he called out to me.

"Hi Todd" I replied then added "I'm almost ready."

"BeeBee…we'll wait for you in the lobby… okay?"

"Don't take too long," cautioned Regina.

"I'll be down in a jiffy guys," I responded and I heard them giggle as they shut the room door after themselves.

I carefully applied my makeup, packed up my cosmetics, put on my earrings and opened the bathroom door. What looked like a four-foot long snake lay across the floor in front of the bathroom door.

"That damn Todd and his silly jokes," I thought as I kicked what I was sure was something Todd, whom I knew was quite the practical joker, had placed there for me. Without a doubt he and Regina were behind the door waiting to crack up at my reaction. As I touched it, the snake slithered in the direction of the bed and disappeared under it. I jumped back. O my God! This is no joke…this is real!

3

When I realized that the snake was real I opened my mouth to scream but no sound came. To get out of the room as quickly as possible I fumbled with the lock of the door, dropping my cosmetics bag on the floor. The door slammed shut behind me. Until I saw other guests coming out of their rooms, their faces contorted in exclamation, I had no idea that that shrill scream I was hearing was actually coming from me.

"A snake's in my room" I yelled.

"A what?"

"Yes... a big snake's in there."

Several persons entered the hallway from their rooms. The occupants of the adjoining room, two middle aged men, looked at me curiously. The door to the room opposite was held slightly ajar by a befrizzled girl with long blue-polished talons. She peered through to see what was causing the ruckus in the hallway. It was only when someone, who looked like a cleaning woman, handed me a sheet to cover myself, I realized I was wearing bra and panties only. No wonder the other people were gaping at me so strangely - they must have thought I was insane.

I don't recall what happened next but the cleaning woman must have phoned the front desk because more motel staff gathered around. Todd and Regina followed behind them.

"What's going on?" Regina asked looking at me with bare feet and wrapped in a bed sheet.

"A snake's in the room" I said again.

"A what?" said Todd. His eyes widened. He was not laughing now.

"Oh God" gasped Regina. She held on to my arm and I could feel her shiver. "How did it get there?"

All my things were still in the room but I certainly wasn't going back in there to get them. We stood in the hallway. A hotel worker went into the room and returned after a few minutes with the snake. I must have fainted when I saw it again.

The motel manager explained that, unknown to the management, the previous occupants had snakes in the room. Upon this discovery, they were ordered to pack up their pets and vacate the premises immediately. What no one realized was that one of those pets had been left behind. The manager reassured the other guests that there would be no further surprises in their rooms.

The management thought the snake might have been hiding in the cot where I slept during the night. I got the creeps just thinking about it. What if it had decided to go for its stroll during the night? What if I had awakened to find it wrapped around me? A thousand 'what ifs' crossed my mind.

To compensate for this frightful experience the motel manager reimbursed us for the room. We were given coupons to pay for our breakfast but my nerves were so shot that morning the last thing I could think of was food.

At the restaurant where we stopped for breakfast, Regina and Todd insisted that I have a cup of herbal tea at the very least to calm me down. Eventually I decided to have a slice of toast as well. Todd was certainly packing it in. I guess I'm like a reformed smoker. Since I've started watching my weight, I am extra sensitive to what people around me eat. Todd had ordered bacon and eggs and ham and sausages, which came with mounds of hash brown potatoes, pancakes and toast.

Before midday we said goodbye to Todd and started the return journey home.

"I'll see you guys soon," he said to us as we departed. He gave us each a little hug. "Take care of yourself BeeBee. I'll be in Ottawa soon."

I was relieved that Regina didn't hold me to my promise that I would do the driving back, so instead I paid for the fill up at the gas station. I was so emotionally drained that I slept most of the journey home.

When I wasn't asleep I thought about that snake in the motel room and shuddered. I remembered when I was a little girl how scared I was of lizards. Harmless as they were, they reminded me of little dinosaurs. I thought of the time when I went to visit my grandmother in the country area of Grenada and someone noticed part of a serpent sticking out from the ceiling boards inside my grandmother's house. Nanny lit a coal pot with some hot peppers and placed it in the room. Everyone left the house and remained outside awaiting the serpent's exit. Apparently serpents are highly sensitive to the peppery smoke. The neighbours all came out to watch the activity. Many of them had cocoa knives on long bamboo sticks in readiness to hook the serpent when it came out. Frozen with fright, I huddled behind my grandmother.

"Look it! Look it! It comin' out now!" someone shouted excitedly. I buried my face in my grandmother's side as I grabbed her around her thick waist.

"I have it," my Uncle Nat armed with a cocoa knife replied.

I didn't want to see but I was relieved when I heard that it was caught and killed. I didn't want to see that either. I was not like my sister Brenda who got a kick out of these sordid activities. She was a year younger than me but nothing seemed to scare her. She didn't mind lizards or congorees or crickets. She would smash a cockroach with her bare foot. I can't count the number of times I was forced to give up a cherished possession because she threatened that if I didn't she would put a congoree down my dress. My mother always said I was the soft one. In fact, I was too soft. She cautioned me that I had to toughen up or else people would walk all over me. But Brenda, she said, was the other extreme. She was a battleaxe just like my father's older sister, whom all of us, even my parents, respectfully called Sister Baby. Mother warned Brenda that you could catch more flies with a drop of honey than with a gallon of vinegar. Brenda simply smiled. She knew that her vinegar was getting her all the flies she wanted - at least from me.

Regina dropped me off at my apartment building before she went to pick up her daughter, whom I knew was waiting feverishly for her mother's return.

"Thanks Reg," I said as I left the car and she sped away.

In the foyer, I picked up my mail from the mailbox. All junk mail, I noticed, with one exception. There was a letter with a Grenada postage stamp from Brenda. On entering my apartment I tossed my weekend bag on the bed before peering into the refrigerator for something to eat. I was famished now. I would read Brenda's letter later. There was a piece of steamed king fish from last week which didn't look too threatening. I decided to reheat it. With some rice which would be ready in five minutes and baby carrots that would be just fine. I tossed out a rotting tomato.

I flicked on the TV while sitting on the living room couch to eat my supper. I opened the letter from Brenda. It was a scant one-pager as usual. A letter from Brenda and no letter were almost equivalent. But while her letters resembled expensive telegrams in which every word cost a fortune, she'd keep you on the phone for hours if you gave her the chance.

Boni,

Coming to visit you during my long leave next March. Mother needs the distraction. Get ready for us.

Hope everything's okay with you.

Brenda.

Succinct and to the point as usual. What did she mean by 'Mother needs the distraction,' I wondered. Well, I would have to phone to find out. After years of scrimping and saving, luckily I was finally in the market for a townhouse as this little one bedroom apartment certainly wouldn't cut it especially if I were to have visitors.

When I was done eating, I placed the empty plate by the side of the couch to join two empty glasses and a bowl already there with the hardened remnants of a last-week's meal. This apartment could do with a thorough cleaning, I thought as I brought my feet up on the couch and closed my eyes. Mother would have a fit if she ever saw the condition of this place. My empty pantry was also in dire need of some groceries. I should walk the couple blocks to the supermarket to pick up a few things. But it would probably be closed by the time I arrived there. I would do that tomorrow after work, I promised myself. Luckily I had picked up my nurse's uniforms from the cleaner's before I left for Toronto with Regina. They were all neatly hanging in my closet, all set for work tomorrow.

As I made myself comfortable on the couch, I thought of that superstitious adage that bad luck happens in threes. Had that just happened to me this week? If that was so then my good luck period or at the very least a period of tranquillity should be kicking in now.

I worked in one of the out-patients' clinics at *Universal* hospital. My hours were the same every day, which I appreciated very much. After ten years working on the wards, shift work had been getting to me and I had been more than ready for a change to the out-patient clinic. But sometimes ambulatory patients could be a real pain in the butt. On the ward where I used to work the patients were too sick to be troublesome. And they were so appreciative - often their gratitude made my day.

These patients were different. Some of them presented quite a challenge. There was one young guy, who came for medical treatment every month and who often caused quite a commotion in the unit. I was scared stiff of him. While I realized that it could be the medication causing him to act out like he did, I nevertheless was extra cautious whenever he was around. The last time he came in for his treatment, he threw a terrible tantrum. Four-letter words spewed loudly from his lips. I was relieved that Mason, my supervisor, was present.

"Oh dear, oh dear" exclaimed Mason in his unique 'mother-hen' way, as he flitted around the desk to retrieve the phone and called the orderly code for help.

Another patient who required time-consuming and costly blood products would call minutes before to cancel an appointment, which had been confirmed and reconfirmed, giving me some 'cock and bull' story. "I'll come in tomorrow," she'd say.

The first time I had to phone the transfusion lab to cancel the product, I learned my lesson. The manager returned my call with a long 'song and dance' about how costly the product was and after its expiration in eight hours it would be wasted. The efforts of Blood Services as well as the transfusion lab, not to mention the donors who gave of their precious time... all these efforts would have been in vain, she said. I didn't know what she expected me to do. Was I supposed to lasso the patient and haul her in? "An incident report will be filed about this," she warned. Frankly, this manager was getting on my nerves. I felt like flipping her the middle finger. I almost told her that I'd put the stuff in my own veins, if that would help. As if it was my fault.

Since then, whenever this patient pulls this stunt, I force her to listen to this whole wastage bit. So far it hasn't had any effect. I have often wondered whether it would have been a good idea to let patients have a periodic record of how much in terms of dollars the system actually put out for them.

The next day as I made my way to the out-patients' clinic, I spotted Adlyn, who worked on the surgical ward. She came towards me with as effervescent a greeting as ever existed. She was all sugar and spice and everything nice.

"Yoh hair lookin' real pretty," she said to me.

I smiled. I wasn't angry with Ad about my hair anymore. As a matter of fact I rather liked my new look.

"And me hear Todd really like you," she grinned mischievously.

"Yeah, yeah" I said thinking the point was...did I really like Todd?

"And me hear all 'bout de woman dat drive her car into de ditch." I nodded. "And..." she took a breath here "de snake." I shuddered. It would be ages before I could get over that experience.

"Don't worry," she said noticing my discomfort. "It wouldn' a' trouble you."

I didn't know how she was so sure of that but I decided not to prolong that topic.

"You bring any lunch today?" she asked as she continued to admire my hair.

"No," I replied and before I could say another word, Ad had taken out a little plastic container from a big tote she carried and put it in my hand.

"Here" she said. "Dis for you."

"For me? Thanks Ad," I said to her undulating backside that was swiftly moving away from me. Without turning around, she waved at me and said "Enjoy."

Looking at the container, I realized I was in for a treat. It contained stewed ox tail and lima beans like Ad and only Ad could make. She may be headstrong and difficult sometimes but, all in all, she was one of the kindest and most generous people I have ever known. She was right up there with Mother and Nanny.

I have an uncanny knack for faces. I may forget names but faces stick with me like a dog after a bone. Many times I catch myself thinking "I've seen that person before...where...where?" I'll think about it for days, sometimes weeks, and eventually it would come to me. That was exactly how I felt when I first met Adlyn Mascoll.

Out of the blue a scene flashed in front of me. It was at the airport in Toronto, many years before. I witnessed an argument between an Air Canada agent and a tall, full-figured lady. The agent looked like she was going to 'pop a vein' in her head any minute. She insisted that both the lady's check-in luggage and hand luggage were over the acceptable limit, and there was no possible way to accommodate a large lampshade, which definitely could not fit below the seat or in the overhead compartment.

Eventually the tall lady gave in and retreated to the ladies' room only to emerge five minutes later with the lampshade stylishly perched on her head. That lady was Adlyn Mascoll.

4

"I'm eleven years old, Aunt Boni," Tiffany blurted out to me. "And Mum still won't let me hang out at the shopping mall with my friends." I was baby sitting Tiffany for Regina who was working late that day. Regina had opted to let Tiffany spend the night with me, so we could work on her English project that was due soon. I was cooking some curried chicken for supper while Tiffany set the table.

"Tiffany, you know your Mum loves you very much and she's doing everything she can for your benefit."

"She doesn't want me to have any fun," Tiffany insisted.

"What?" I almost dropped the potato I was peeling.

"She goes out all the time but she doesn't want me going out and having any fun," whined Tiffany.

"Sorry...but who was it that went to Disney World last March break?"

Tiffany remained silent.

"And who just got a brand new bedroom set for her birthday?" I thought I'd score a touchdown for Regina, whom I imagined must have overextended herself considerably to make that purchase.

Tiffany frowned.

"That's fine Aunt Boni, but..."

"I would say that's very fine indeed."

"But all my friends can go and hang out at the mall. I'm the only one that can't go."

"Your mother wants you to be safe, Tiff."

"I'm not going to do anything wrong but Mum just doesn't trust me," Tiffany moaned.

"Tiffany, you have to earn your mother's trust," I said. "And gradually she'll give you more and more freedom and responsibility. But you have to show her that you're ready."

I saw the whole scene clearly. It was important for Tiffany to hang out with her friends at the mall. But Regina was deathly scared of some of the misdeeds children Tiffany's age were already getting into. We'd all heard the rumour of the group that skipped classes to hang out in an empty house, smoking, drinking and engaging in sex. Regina didn't want this for her daughter but it was difficult explaining this to Tiffany.

"And now I can't even see my Daddy anymore. Mum told him not to come back to visit."

"Whaat?" I didn't think Regina realized that the paper thin walls of her apartment had afforded Tiffany a front row seat in the big fight she told me she and Michael had the last time he visited. Now while she was cast in the role of dragon, Michael was 'dear Daddy' in their daughter's eyes. "I'm sure you can go visit your father sometimes."

"He didn't even call me for my birthday," Tiffany whimpered.

As if that was Regina's fault. But I realized that Tiffany was hurt and the parent that was present was likely to get the brunt of her resentment. Unfair but whoever said life was fair?

After a supper of curried chicken encased in roti - one of Tiffany's favorites - I suggested we walk over to the library to work on her project.

"Walk? Why we can't take the bus? I don't want to walk." When Tiffany was in her whining mood, everything was a problem. I was already getting into my running shoes, which were on the mat by the door next to hers.

"It's much faster to walk, Tiff. Trust me." Ever since my old, ailing Chevy gave out on me last year, I'd been walking just about everywhere. Work was only twenty minutes away, so even in the winter I could manage that. Before I realized it, the pounds were slipping off my oversized body slowly but surely. I was in no hurry to replace my car, until I got Brenda's letter, telling me of her plan for herself and Mother to come visit me during her long leave vacation next year.

Reluctantly, Tiffany put on her running shoes and followed me out the door. At the library, we got several books on Florence Nightingale. I also included a few on Mary Secole.

"Who's she?" asked Tiffany.

"You've never heard of her?"

"Nope."

That's what I had thought. In her project on Florence Nightingale, I deliberately wanted Tiffany to include mention of Mary Secole, a black woman of Jamaican descent, who like Nightingale also practiced nursing in the Crimean war. Her reputation as a skillful nurse and healer earned her much respect. Despite Nightingale's overt discrimination towards her, Secole became as important in the war as Nightingale. Somehow Mary Secole seemed to have slipped through the cracks of history.

Tiffany's interest in her project suddenly mushroomed forth. "Oooh...this is so cool," she said as she made notes on an index card about Mary Secole. I smiled inwardly. Finally the whining child was giving way to the bright, interesting child again. The time flew by. We were among the last to leave the library at closing time.

I made a mental note to talk to Regina about the conversation Tiffany and I had today. I would suggest that if she did well on her project and I knew she would, her mother reward her by allowing her to hang out at the mall with her friends. We could agree on a time period and I would volunteer to take her and pick her up at an agreed upon time and place in the mall. I knew it would be a hard sell but I was willing to go batting for Tiffany.

Todd called me when he arrived in Ottawa. He said he was staying with a friend. No... It wasn't Ad and Herbert. They had invited him over for dinner on Saturday. He wondered whether he could drop by my apartment that evening since his friend was busy. I was busy too, I said and I hardly socialize during the week. The disappointment in his voice prompted me to soften, and I invited him to come over for supper on Friday. He sounded relieved.

"Good BeeBee" he said gleefully. "See you then." I wondered whether he was here on business. I remembered Regina mentioning that she thought he was in sales.

I couldn't believe it. Todd was trying to sell me a vacuum cleaner. He was a vacuum cleaner salesman and I guess he thought he'd branch out into Ottawa from Toronto. He spent the past half hour cleaning my couch and drapery and using an attachment to rake in the dirt from difficult to clean areas.

"That's a real good deal Todd" I lied, "but since I don't have any carpets I'm not about to spend that kind of money on a vacuum cleaner now."

"But BeeBee you want to see all the dirt that this cleaner vacuumed up?"

I didn't but I knew he was going to show me anyway. I felt like I was trapped in the seat of a dental hygienist, who was chiding me for not flossing properly.

"Wow!" I tried to seem impressed. "You mean my couch was that dirty!"

He went into a long harangue about allergens and stuff that lay hidden ready to kill you if you didn't buy his damned vacuum cleaner. And I was getting a big discount and a set of steak knives - I didn't eat steak - if I signed up right away. I could tell he was regurgitating all the junk he had picked up from his training session.

I excused myself and went into the kitchen to prepare a green salad. When Todd called a few days ago to ask if he could pass in for a visit, I stupidly assumed it was a social visit and invited him to have supper with me. I didn't think he was coming with a sales pitch that I was definitely not interested in.

Minutes later we sat down to supper, which was meatballs and spaghetti with a green salad. Since I couldn't discreetly switch the wine glasses on the table for water glasses I opened the bottle of *chablis* as I had planned.

"You have any rice?" Todd asked looking in the direction of the kitchen. Obviously he wasn't particularly keen on the fare before him. I had even added a basket of sliced garlic bread. I did not hide the frown on my face.

"Why? What's wrong with spaghetti?"

Todd grimaced. "Sorry BeeBee... I should have warned you... I don't eat pasta."

"Well you can have more of the bread then." If he thought I was going to cook rice now he was mistaken.

"Show me where the rice is and I'll cook some. It don't take long."

This fellow was beginning to irritate me.

"I don't have any rice," I said. Actually I had some brown rice but something told me he was not a brown rice kind of person.

Todd guffawed but there was a sarcastic tinge to it.

"You're the first Caribbean woman I know who don't have rice in her kitchen," he said as he helped himself to meatballs and bread.

"Don't let me force you... feel free to take yourself to a restaurant if you wish," I answered crisply. First he tries to sell me a stupid vacuum cleaner, next he complains about my food. One more incident and I was going to throw his backside to the curb. I think Todd sensed my annoyance with him, as he made a big deal to patch things up, complimenting my meatballs. He even tried a bit of spaghetti.

"There... it didn't kill you... did it?"

"Not yet," he said grimacing.

Things improved slightly after this. I learned that Todd had been a teacher working up in northern Ontario. He had applied for leave to do his Master's degree but was denied, even though he was prepared to take it without pay. He therefore quit his job in frustration. But after completing his MA, it seemed impossible for him to get back into teaching. He spent two years in Ottawa doing substitute teaching, he said. He was told constantly that he was too qualified. "Based on my qualifications and experience, I would have to be paid at the top of the scale," said Todd. "And there was no way that was going to happen." I had a feeling Todd was embellishing this story slightly but I felt sympathetic towards him. And now he was selling vacuum cleaners? Something was wrong with this picture.

"Yes BeeBee," he continued with a smirk. "Last hired... first fired!"

My mind drifted to a story Regina's friend Veronique, who worked as a secretary for a big company in Montreal, had related to her. She had overheard her boss talking on the phone one day, saying what remarkable qualifications some candidate had for a certain position. "I've never seen anything like it," he'd said and one moment later "but unfortunately we can't send guys like this out there in the field to represent us. Maybe if we had something inside..." Just as Veronique had suspected, this candidate was black. I shook my head sadly as I looked over at Todd but said nothing. It would sound so much like an empty cliché if I told him that he had to keep on keeping on.

I served a fruit salad for dessert. I could tell Todd would have preferred a dessert laced with calories but accepted my fresh fruit salad.

"I should eat like this more often" he said.

"Like what?"

"Fruit and salads and stuff... I'll sure lose some pounds if I ate like this more often," he said as he caressed his bulging stomach.

"Oh well...something's bound to kill us sometime...if it's not clogged arteries, then maybe it's allergens." It was my turn to laugh as Todd looked rather tongue in cheek.

As he helped me bring the used dishes to the kitchen, the rest of his agenda began to unfold. "You know BeeBee" he said intently, "ever since I met you ... I been dreaming of you practically every night."

"Well now you'll be dreaming of bad food and dirt." I tried to make light of what he'd said.

"No BeeBee... I'm dead serious... ever since I met you... I can't stop thinking of you."

What a lame line. I wanted to say I knew that ever since he'd met me he'd been thinking here's a donkey he could dump a vacuum cleaner on. I smiled. "Come on Todd... we're just getting to know each other... you hardly know me."

"I like what I see though."

"Trust me... there's more to me than what you see."

It was my first break for the day. Francine, another nurse in the clinic where I worked, had called in sick and there was no replacement. It was short-staffed in the unit as usual. Even though Mason had told me to take a long break, I knew he would appreciate seeing me back as soon as possible. So after I finished my bowl of watery onion soup and sandwich in the coffee shop, I took the escalator back to the unit.

"*Ma chèrie*... back already?" said Mason as he promptly handed me a file, with the name Jacqueline Dacota. He wiped sweat from his forehead with the back of his hand. A few strands of hair lay across his glistening scalp. "Here... Mrs. Dacota is in room 2. Can you finish her?" He was obviously relieved that I was back so soon. There were several patients awaiting attention.

I took the file from Mason, returned my purse to the bottom drawer of my desk and as I hastened into room 2, checked the file to see what was required.

"Mrs. Dacota?" I said as I entered the room. She turned to face me and that familiar 'bird crap' splash, identical to the one sported by Russian President Gorbachev, stared at me from her forehead. That was the woman whose car had gone into the ditch, missing Regina's car by a hair. So that was her name - Jacqueline Dacota. I was dying to ask her how her little boy was and how things went after the ditch incident. I remembered she'd told me she was having a difficult time. But in this business confidentiality is essential so I remained silent. I took her vital signs, which I entered in her file. I then noted her upcoming date of surgery and retrieved and filled out the relevant forms, which I then gave her to take to the blood lab, to have her blood work done. "This is indeed a small world," I said to myself.

5

I was in the market for a new car. Since Mother and Brenda were coming to visit, I might as well get one sooner rather than later. My original intention was first of all to move into a townhouse, which with Adlyn's encouragement and direction I had purchased and which was to be built at the south side of the city. Once I'd moved in and settled in, I would start my research on a car. But now I had to rearrange my plans a bit. I spoke to my banker who agreed to consolidate both loans. As usual, I began doing a lot of research on different types and brands of cars. I intended to get the very best bargain that was possible out there. My bed as well as my worn couch and coffee table soon became a sea with all kinds of brochures.

In a phone call to Brenda, she said that Mother was going through a period of listlessness. This holiday was an attempt to pull her out of it. She would have something to look forward to and then of course the visit itself.

"She's suffering from empty nest syndrome," Brenda divulged. Five years ago Brenda had finally and permanently moved out of our parents' home. Less than a month later my father suffered a heart attack and passed away. I had gone on a camping retreat that weekend with my co-workers and when I returned to my little apartment, I received the frantic news from my mother and Brenda who had been calling non-stop since the day before. The very next day I was on board a plane on my way home to Grenada.

It seemed that every time I had planned a vacation at home, something had intervened to cancel it, so this was my first return visit to Grenada after more than twelve years. Too bad it had to be under such sad circumstances. Too bad too it had been so rushed and I didn't have time to get my hair professionally done and to prepare that compulsory, knock-'em-dead wardrobe carefully planned to propagate that myth of prosperity in the adopted country. After all, what would be the point of living in that cold place if one wasn't at least better off economically. Heeding Adlyn's advice I had crammed as much as I could into a carry-on bag, my only luggage, not daring to risk arriving in Grenada while my luggage remained in limbo somewhere else.

I arrived three hours before the funeral. Brenda met me at the airport. She had blossomed into a fine-looking, stylish young woman. I felt rather frumpy in her presence. She took me right away to the funeral parlor to visit Father. Memories of my father during my growing up years were scant. He always seemed to be away working or, if at home, hidden behind a newspaper. While not overbearing he was certainly not affectionate. Nevertheless as I stared at his lifeless body, I was overcome by a deep sense of sadness; a sense of precious time lost, which could never ever be regained.

At home after Mother and I embraced and I held her across from me, I noticed she looked tired and worn. Soft wrinkles bracketed her eyes. I could tell the events of the past few days had been hard on her and I pulled her to me again. However, she demonstrated her old take-charge get-down-to-business self as a short while later she returned from her bedroom with a folder of papers, which she deposited in my lap, instructing me that I was to deliver the eulogy at the church. It was less than two hours before the funeral.

"You could use some o' dis stuff if you want," she added.

As I thumbed through the contents of the folder, I looked hopelessly across at Brenda. There were innumerable church and school certificates, information on societies my father belonged to, conferences attended over the years and medals and ribbons and diplomas obtained, political party speeches, information on his parents – everything I concluded but the names of family pets. My head ached looking at all this stuff. I was beginning to feel overwhelmed when Brenda saved the day. She handed me a single type written page on which she had written a eulogy of my father.

"This is great," I said with obvious relief after I'd read it. It was brief, poignant and uplifting, without being overdone. "But why don't you read it yourself?" Brenda was adamant. "No...no. You do it," she said as she shook her head. "I'm gwine just break down and cry if I start to read this." Brenda had been much closer to Father than I had been. "Besides," she teeheed, "Mother want to show off your new accent."

I remained with my mother and sister for the rest of the week after the funeral. I visited relatives in the country and retraced my childhood haunts. Nanny's old house had been replaced by a potato patch. So many of the older people I used to know had passed away. Uncle Nat and his wife, Aunt Sybil, were showing signs of 'getting down' and when we bade one another goodbye, they reminded me that this might be our last farewell. I was feeling disheartened and sad and that infernal question by many people who dropped by to visit did not help in the least. "So Boni...yoh not married or anyt'ing? No children?" they would ask me with a 'poor you' look on their faces. I felt judgmental eyes scrutinizing my appearance and concluding that prosperity had certainly eluded me despite many years abroad. I was beginning to feel like a failure in their eyes. It was not without some relief that I finally boarded the plane on my return journey to the cold place.

"How come Mother suffering from empty nest syndrome?" I now asked Brenda, "when MLP got dozens of children running through that house all the time?" I exaggerated a bit referring to Uncle Nat's daughter Patty, whom we nicknamed Minister of Labour and Production or MLP for short and her brood of children who recently moved near to Mother's.

"Yes... but she want her own grandchildren," Brenda snickered.

"Well... get cracking then," I teased Brenda.

Brenda laughed. "I'm waiting for you... first come, first start."

"Sure" I said sarcastically. I never wanted to admit that of the two of us Mother showed a slight preference for me. Ninety nine percent of the time, Brenda and I were treated exactly the same. But there was that one percent - it was weird but something that Brenda just took in stride. Bless her heart. I don't know how I would have reacted had it been the other way around.

We both graduated from high school the same year. Following in our mother's footsteps we both wanted to become nurses. Without a question I was the one sent abroad to study while Brenda pursued her training at the colony hospital at home.

"We can only afford to send one," Mother had explained to me and I never questioned her further. I was after all the older one and since Brenda was deeply in love with her childhood sweetheart, it was in her interest to remain in Grenada where he was. It bothered me to hear that Mother was feeling down now and I decided to do whatever I could to lift her spirits.

My mother had three older brothers - Uncle Dawson, now dead, Uncle Benny and Uncle Nat. Between them - Uncle Benny and Uncle Nat had ten children and twice as many grandchildren. The rumour mill knowledgeably declared that Uncle Dawson, who went to England long before I was born and died there, had just as many children there too. I had so many cousins that the fact that I had only one sister did not matter in the least.

Nanny, my mother's mother was a robust, independent woman despite her age. She used to live in Côte St. Pierre in the northern part of the island, not far from the famous Leaper's Hill; a steep cliff that descends vertically into the sea for more than one hundred feet. History informs us that that was where the Kalinago, who were the original inhabitants of the island, after suffering a series of losing battles to the French, many of them jumped to their death, preferring suicide to domination by the French.

I enjoyed spending my school vacations with Nanny. On most occasions I went alone and Brenda simply stayed home. It never occurred to me that that was unfair to Brenda. After all, Nanny's small house could only accommodate one of us and since I was the older one - ah well - someone had to stay to help Mother.

Uncle Nat and his wife, Aunt Sybil, lived next door to Nanny's with their three youngest children - Clyde, Lucille and Henry. Although crippled from birth, Clyde gained the respect and fear of the neighbourhood children because of his strong arms, surpassed only by his accuracy with stone throwing. Nobody troubled Clyde because if he wasn't able to get hold of the culprit, a stone was sure to connect with that person's head with absolute precision.

Lucille, a sweet girl, who obeyed me for most of her pre-teen life, was the sister I wished I had in Brenda. Even at that young age, she performed miracles on my thick, unruly mop of hair, turning out the most intricate and beautiful cornrows and braids I'd ever seen.

Everyone called Henry 'Stonehead' because to his mother's chagrin, he did everything his own way - he never listened to what anyone said. "You such ah stonehead," Aunt Sybil would say in exasperation and the name eventually stuck. They all made a big fuss over me whenever I arrived from St. George's and I loved it.

Electricity did not exist in Nanny's home then. Yet there was something romantic about her lighting the lamps as it grew dark in the evenings. Catching crayfish in the river with my cousins and other children in the village was high on my list of adventures. I even enjoyed those days when Nanny washed the dirty clothes at the standpipe near her gap. She would join two or three other women already there with their tubs and wash boards.

"Hi Doux Doux" they would say to me kindly as they slapped and rubbed the clothes on their wash boards. I admired the squishing sound that they got the clothes to make as they rubbed them together in their hands but as hard as I tried I was never able to replicate that sound.

Uncle Benny, Aunt Theresa and their four children lived over on Sunlight Hill, in the adjoining parish of the famous Grand Etang - a lake situated in the crater of an extinct volcano and believed to be connected underground to the harbour in St. George's, several miles away. Some folks told stories of how they witnessed a bubbling up of the Grand Etang, when a volcano in a neighbouring Windward island began erupting. With the exception of Uncle Benny, no one from this family ever visited Côte St. Pierre, so I never got to know them well. "Theresa an' Sybil don' mix," Nanny once responded to one of my many inquiries. "Dey like oil an' vinegar."

In retrospect, those childhood days in the country with Nanny were heavenly. Despite constant warnings from Mother that I should always wear my shoes - "Don' go and get no jigger foot," she warned - I walked around bare-footed, swam in the river daily with my cousins, and brushed my teeth when I remembered. Nanny never bothered to check on such inconsequential details. Aunt Sybil, who was quite the disciplinarian, often complained that while Nanny used to be deadly strict with her own children, with the grandchildren, especially me, she was a big pushover.

Sometimes Lucille and I would go down the road to buy chewing gum at Mr. Hanson's shop. This was the most fancy building in the village. Two empty show windows jutted out on either side of a door, over which a huge sign proudly proclaimed 'Hansonville.' Mr. Hanson had spent the greater part of his life in the United States and upon retirement had returned with an American drawl to his homeland, built a modern home, complete with fake fireplace and set up a beautiful but empty shop next door. On entering the shop, one had to shout loudly to get Mr. Hanson's attention as he was almost always in the back room or at his home next door. The sudden barking of his dog, when anyone entered the store, usually got his attention. Interestingly enough, residents swore that the dog also had a Yankee accent. Its bark was definitely different from those of other neighbourhood dogs.

"Just a minute," Mr. Hanson's deep voice would reply. About twenty minutes later, aided by his cane, he would slowly emerge into the store.

"Hello," he would say. I loved his deep melodic voice and the way he dragged out the last syllable forever.

"A stick o' peppermint chewin' gum... please sah," Lucille would say. Apart from the chewing gum, try as we might, there wasn't a single other item Lucille and I could find to buy in that shop.

In stark contrast to Mr. Hanson's shop was Mr. Izzy's further down the road. It was a small store but every inch was taken up with items of some kind. All kinds of goods hung from the ceiling - belts, shoes, pots and pans, doormats, everything. Prominently displayed on the counter, next to jars of 'Extra Strong' mints was a jar of leeches for whoever had bad blood or some infection. Just leave it to the leeches. Mr. Izzy would readily produce items such as Zubes Cough Syrup or Canadian Healing Oil from behind the counter. If you needed a particular bolt or screw, he was sure to have it. In that jumble, he seemed to know where each and every item was. When faced with the dilemma of not being able to find a particular grade of twine in St. George's for our kites, with kite season fast approaching, Mr. Izzy's store came to the rescue.

There was much to do and learn in the country. Unknown to Nanny, who might have worried about me getting hurt and the predicament my parents would be thrown into, I actively participated in many activities such as tree-climbing, which my father would have considered 'unladylike'. That there was quite an art to this, I unfortunately discovered the hard way. Some trees were best avoided. The deceptively sturdy looking limbs of the plum tree in Uncle Nat's back yard would give way instantly if one were to put his or her weight on them.

Then there were Uncle Nat's two donkeys - Tutsy and Bubber, whose temperaments differed as night from day. Tutsy was kind and mild mannered - even a baby could ride her but Bubber presented a much greater challenge. He could be very moody. Of course my cousins took up that challenge and invited me to do likewise. Lucille and Stonehead, who were both younger than me, fearlessly tackled Bubber. I witnessed the time when Bubber took off at high speed with Stonehead on his back. He made straight for the clothesline with

Stonehead ducking in the nick of time before he could be decapitated. I didn't want to be thought of as the 'softie' from St. George's so I reluctantly agreed to get on Bubber's back. When he headed at full speed to an area with sharp, prickly patches of 'boisbuck' and deposited me smack in the middle of it, I decided I'd had enough. If the world ever appreciated how intelligent these animals were the word 'asinine' would surely take on a new meaning.

Most of all I loved the fruit and the food at Nanny's. There was a prolific sugar apple tree in Nanny's front yard, which was well known to bear the sweetest sugar apples for miles around. If you wanted a delicious mango you had to go no further than the Sheboh mango tree behind Teacher Angela's pigpen. Then no one - not even Mother - cooked like Nanny. I usually returned to town after my vacation well rounded and bursting out of my clothes.

Much to my parents' dismay, I would return with a country twang as well. When a day after I had returned from the country they heard me saying to Brenda "Leh we go veesit Jeem's food store. Ah fil to it ah pis o' chiz" my mother was appalled.

"For heaven sake Boni... you can speak better dan dat!" she shouted at me.
My father looked up from reading the newspaper.

"You know Rebecca... I don' know why you keep sendin' her in the country. Every time she come back more and more country-booky."
My mother gave my father 'the eye'. I knew she wanted to 'take a bite off him' but not in front of us.

"Jus' dat it so crowded 'round here Denis...you know... an' Mama love havin' her an' she love it there too" she said softly.

My father worked as a sanitary inspector. His job took him all over the island, occasionally to nearby islands, sometimes for days on end. Whenever my father wasn't around, I assumed he was working. My father's parents lived with us, or rather we lived with them in a small bungalow, until they both passed away while I was still quite young. I was about fifteen before I discovered that my grandparents owned the home in which we lived.

At one time my father's sister, Sister Baby, moved in with us. She definitely favored Brenda over me and made no secret of that fact. She complained that I was lazy and selfish and if my parents didn't watch out, I was fast becoming a hooligan. I recall a time when Brenda accidentally knocked down a vase of flowers on the living room table while chasing me with a caterpillar she was threatening to put down my dress. Sister Baby was furious and blasted into me. To no avail did I point out that it was Brenda and not me that had broken the vase. Sister Baby insisted that I was the older one and should have known better than to carry our silly games inside the house. Everyone seemed to treat Sister Baby with kid's gloves. No one argued with her. I never understood those dynamics but I knew better than to question them. I'd certainly be told that was none of my business.

Nanny and Uncle Nat always claimed that I was lucky to be here because my mother almost checked out long before her time. Neither of them cared to go further with that story until one day, sucking sugar cane on the stoop in front of Nanny's house, Uncle Nat took it an inch further.

"Is more dan one time, yoh mudder almos' check out an' leave us," he said to me.

"Mmhmmm" agreed Nanny.

"Yes?" I was all ears.

"De Lord sho is good," continued Uncle Nat, looking at me as he shook his head appreciatively. "We never t'ought we would a' see dis day."

"Mmhmmm," said Nanny again. I waited intently. But instead of continuing with the story, Nanny pointed to a juicy looking piece of sugar cane and said to Uncle Nat, "Why you don' split dat nice piece o' cane dey for de children."

About an hour later, my belly full of sugar cane, it dawned on me that I never heard the rest of the story.

Consequently I decided to go directly to the source - my mother. Mother simply rolled her eyes and shook her head. "That's a long story, Bunny... and you too young to hear about it." I figured it had something to do with childbirth. I decided that my mother probably almost died giving birth to me or to Brenda. That had to be it. There was so much I wanted to know about my family but it was either none of my business or I was too young to hear about it.

6

Before leaving for Canada, I spent a week in the country with Nanny. She was ninety years old but still as astute and active as ever. We bonded even more closely during that period, when we both sensed, although it remained unspoken, that this could be our last time together. She told me many family stories including the mysterious ones, about when my mother almost checked out long before her time.

The year was 1944, she said, as we sat together on two hard wooden chairs underneath the sugar apple tree in her front yard. My mother was eighteen years old. With a group of young people, she was planning a trip up the islands on board the famous ship - *The Island Queen*. For months all the young people in the parish talked about was this planned cruise to the other windward islands. Rebecca, my mother, had never been so happy. She was looking forward to spending some time with a certain young man, in romantic surroundings.

"Whaat?...Was that Daddy?" I interrupted Nanny as I leaned forward in my chair, elbows on my knees.

"Never min' dat," said Nanny sternly as she continued the story. I had a feeling Nanny still saw me as a little child and not the nineteen-year old young woman that I was then.

The stage had been set for an exciting holiday full of gaiety and partying. But Nanny had a bad feeling about this trip. For several nights she'd been having a recurring dream about washing dirty clothes in dirty water. Whenever she dreamt about dirty clothes and dirty water, that was an ominous sign.

"Yes," said Nanny. "I know dat was ah bad sign." She squeezed her eyes shut. Then opening them again continued "I din know what to do... so I jus' take it to de Lord in prayer."

The morning of the cruise my mother woke up covered with blemishes all over her body. She had contracted glass pox. "There was no way she could a' go on dis trip. She couldn'a even go near nobody. We was quarantine," said Nanny. "Rebecca was so upset... she cry so much... I t'ought she po' heart would a' break open" said Nanny. "If anyt'ing else had happen to her... a fever or belly pain... she would a' still go. But everybody know dat wid de pox you an' everybody else 'round you mus' be quarantine."

When the clock in the front room struck twelve and Rebecca knew that *The Island Queen* was on its way, she became more and more miserable. The first stop was St. Vincent. "I know dat de mo' Rebecca t'ink 'bout de happy, laughin' faces on board de *Island Queen*, de mo' miserable she get."

Just listening to Nanny relating this story gave me goose bumps.

"Eh Eh…" said Nanny. "Dat nex' evenin' I dey sittin' down doin' a little mendin', when I hear Benny in de gap calling out to me.

'Mama… you hear what happen?'

'Don' come down here Benny… Rebecca have de pox,' I call back out to him quickly.

'I know Mama. Say t'anks to de Lord Mama for givin' Rebecca pox, as it save she life.'

'What?'"

Uncle Benny told Nanny the news that *The Island Queen* never arrived in St. Vincent. No one knew what happened on the high seas. It had simply disappeared. By then several neighbours had gathered around Uncle Benny in the gap, all wondering what had happened to the ship, its passengers and crew. Was it a storm? There was no evidence of that. Was it caused by the volcanic activity of Kick 'em Jenny? Hardly likely as experienced sailors knew well how to avoid that rough and dangerous area of the sea, just north of Grenada. Some radio news reporters speculated that it was friendly fire from a British submarine, that mistook *The Island Queen*, which had a new German engine, for an enemy target. After all, it was wartime. But the sad fact was that all the people on board were lost.

"Oh Gawd!" someone exclaimed and Nanny turned around to see Rebecca, eyes staring as if she'd just seen a ghost. Almost all her friends and her young man were on that cruise. She couldn't believe it. "Oh Gawd!" she cried again before she collapsed on the floor.

Families were beyond distraught. Some had lost several of their young people. The emotional toll on mothers, fathers, brothers, sisters, relatives was huge. One poor woman lost her only child on this boat. It seemed that she too wasn't going to make it. The entire island mourned.

Rebecca was numb. Long after she recovered from the glass pox, she remained in a state of shock.

"I look at po' Rebecca," Nanny said, "an' I try tell her dat was jus' de will o' de Lord. I say 'God have somet'ing plan for you to do darlin' an' it jus' wasn' yoh time yet'." Nanny remained quiet for a while then looking at me added "Remember dat Boni, God have somet'ing plan for every one of us. We could take it or leave it."

I didn't get the full significance of this plan Nanny was talking about but I felt sorry for Mother. Now I understood why she never wanted to talk about that incident. It would push all those painful memories to the surface again. I wondered whether she'd gotten over that event or at least made peace with it. I decided that some day I'd talk to her about it.

I was happy that after all these years I was finally learning some of the family stories.

"Thanks Nanny" I said. "Thanks for telling me."

I spent that week in the country with Nanny doing all the things I enjoyed most as a child. I felt a sense of nostalgia. Sometimes I wished I had the power to stop the clock. I recalled that Biblical saying - 'when I became a man I put away the things of a child.' But I didn't want to. It was time to move on, I told myself reluctantly. That's the way of life.

Nanny found a way to make all my favorite dishes that week. One morning before I could go to the kitchen to help with breakfast, an aromatic whiff of cinnamon floated into the bedroom. I went out to investigate. On the kitchen table was a bowl of my favorite - hot corn porridge topped with cinnamon and brown sugar. I looked at Nanny and the tears sprung to my eyes.

"What happen...you don' like corn porridge no mo'?"
I knew this was her way of arresting my tears and maybe hers as well. I hugged her.
"Of course I do Nanny... I love it."

Both Nanny and I enjoyed taking long walks at night, when there was no hot sun to burn the skin, which was instead caressed by the coolness of the night's breeze. Whether it was a dark night or a moonlit night, we simply enjoyed it.

As a child, when I first arrived from St. George's with its brightly lit streets, I was struck by the total blackness of the nights in Côte St. Pierre. Try as I might I couldn't see a single thing in the dark. I might as well have been blindfolded. Holding Nanny's arm tightly, I was led like a blind person. Suddenly out of the darkness, someone would say "Night Ma Bennett" and Nanny would answer "Night Sam" or "Night Teacher Angela" without missing a beat. It was a mystery to me how they recognized one another. But after a week or two in the country I was doing the same myself. My eyes and ears got used to the dark. From many yards away my ear would pick up Mr. Hanson's laboured gait with his walking stick long before he came into full view. And I couldn't understand how I could have failed to recognize the rocking motion of Hop an' Drop Sam.

Sometimes though, the moonlight can play tricks with your vision; especially after it rained. As older teenagers, my cousin Lucille and I were returning home late one night, when we saw what looked like a very tall person right at the split of the road, a section where we were obliged to pass to get to our homes.

"Look...what's dat?" I grabbed Lucille's arm and we both stopped.

"Shhh" said Lucille as she held me tightly. I could feel her tension. "It look like *La Diablesse*."
I was skeptical although my heart began to beat quickly. Mother had convinced me that those things existed only in the minds of superstitious people. *La Diablesse* was supposedly a very tall, treacherous and hypnotizing woman, who came out at night wearing a long dress concealing one cow's foot and one human foot. Legend had it that many men were tricked to their death following her off dangerous cliffs.

"Don' be so stupid girl... dat's no *La Diablesse*'" I chided Lucille as I boldly decided to go past it, but still holding Lucille tightly. We were about ten tentative yards away when the strange apparition lurched towards us. Like a bolt of lightning we took off in the opposite direction. Sweat was pouring down my back as my thumping heart threatened to break open my chest cavity. Poor Lucille was prupsing away like a car back firing.

For the next half an hour we summoned up our courage and made a few more attempts to go past this 'thing'. On one occasion it turned around suddenly, brandishing what I was sure was a sword or a huge cutlass. I knew Nanny and Aunt Sybil must be wondering why we hadn't returned home yet. We could detour through Hop an' Drop Sam's back yard but it would be hell to pay if we trampled anything in his kitchen garden but even worse was his big, bad dog, which would surely shred us to bits if it wasn't tied.

Finally we heard someone coming from the bottom road. Clutching each other tightly, we watched as this person passed the supposed *La Diablesse* quite safely and then realized with relief that the person was none other than Nanny. She was coming to look for us.

"Nanny!" Lucille and I shouted at the same time as we rushed forward to her.

"What y'all doin' here? Y'all suppose to be home long time." Nanny scolded us harshly. I could tell she was relieved. We resolutely walked with Nanny past the source of our terror. I began to laugh nervously. That was no *La Diablesse*. It was only a leaf from a wet banana tree swaying eerily in the wind with the light of the moon reflecting off it.

7

During one of our long night walks that final week I spent with Nanny, I learned from her the story of that infamous night when I came into this world. It was infamous not because of me but because it was the night of the disastrous Hurricane Janet. I never understood, until Nanny told me, all the drama that surrounded my birth.

My mother went into labour around three o' clock that afternoon in September 1955 two weeks earlier than expected. Nanny had planned to come to St. George's to stay with her around the time of her confinement. Usually first babies are late so it was agreed that Nanny wouldn't come until the expected week of delivery.

Nanny paused for a moment, as we moved to the side of the road to allow an oncoming car to pass by, then continued relating the story. "Rebecca slip on a piece o' mango skin in de yard an' take a bad fall dat mornin'. I t'ink dat's what bring on de labour so soon." Because a hurricane warning was in effect that day schools were closed early and people were sent home early from work. "Loudspeakers pass up and down de street warnin' people of de expected hurricane." Most people disregarded these warnings, having heard them so many times before, when no hurricane came. Buses stopped running. Phone lines were down making it impossible to get word to Nanny in the country that Rebecca was in labour and even if that was doable it would be useless. There was no transportation as by that time the roads were becoming impassable.

"Denis decide he bringin' Rebecca to de hospital to have de baby...by den de pains lickin' her down plenty. But jus' openin' de front door was one big fight wid de wind. I have to t'ank Papa and Mama Burke.

'No way' Papa Burke say. 'If dis baby comin', it gwine come right here and all of us gwine help Rebecca.' Rebecca look at Mama Burke, who understan' well what she t'inkin'. Makin' baby is woman business and men don' ha' no business dey."

I listened intently. Nanny was quite the storyteller. I wished I was taping all of this.

"By ten o' clock in de night de wind get so strong, all de windows an' doors rattlin' like steel drum as water pourin' in from de tiniest little crack." Nanny's bed was soaked. The house was like one big sieve. "We get out de big plastic sheet and all o' we; Nat, Sybil wid Clyde who was jus' a little baby, Gabe, Donald and Patty; we all sit down on de wet floor underneat' it. I say to Nat 'I hope Rebecca okay. She near she time you know.' Nat say 'you always t'inkin' 'bout Rebecca... I hope we make it t'rough dis night, Mama.' Jus' as he say dat, I hear ah loud PADDOW outside an' de whole house shake. Dat was de breadfruit tree dat fall down an' swipe de side o' de house. De main stem miss de house by ah kmm. Nat almos' jump out he skin. Sybil start to bawl. She an' all de children frighten, frighten, frighten. But I couldn'a stop t'inkin' 'bout Rebecca. I close me eyes an' start to pray over an' over 'Spare us O Lord, spare thy people and be not angry wid us forever'. You won' believe how dat prayer help me."

    In St. George's, Rebecca and Denis with Papa and Mama Burke faired no better. Electricity was cut off. The house rattled and shook as though some invisible giant was determined to topple it over. As the wind attacked viciously and vehemently, one could hear loud crashing, banging and hurling outside. Rebecca lay on a cot, which was pushed to the only dry section of the house - the kitchen. Searing pain ripped through her back forcing her to add her screams to the commotion outside.

    Mama Burke held her hand. She didn't know whether the terror she felt was due to the hurricane or the fact that she was convinced that Rebecca's baby was coming the wrong way. It was breach. She had witnessed the delivery of many babies and she knew well that that situation was serious. It meant they might lose both mother and child.

    "How she doin' Mammy?" Denis asked his mother as he entered the kitchen. Despite the flickering of the lamp, terror stared at him from his mother's eyes, as looking at Rebecca, she shook her head slowly from side to side. Denis took Rebecca's hand and squeezed it. He bent down to kiss her cheek and realized she was trying to say something. He listened attentively and caught a bit of a familiar prayer. He joined her unashamedly and loudly. "Spare us O Lord, Spare thy people and be not angry with us forever." Papa Burke came into the kitchen at that time and both himself and

Mama Burke joined in the prayer, first chanting, then singing with the roaring of the wind, the lashing rain and Rebecca's moans all merged together in background accompaniment. Eventually they were all overcome by a strange sense of peace. They felt that through all this God would guide and protect them.

It was Papa Burke who quietly and calmly made the decision to operate on Rebecca. "I done it many times before... it easy," he insisted.

"You done dis before?" Mama Burke looked at him with disbelief.

"Yes... wid sheep an' goat" explained Papa Burke. "Same t'ing."

"Anyhow," went on Nanny. "Papa Burke sterilize he sharpest knife an' Mama Burke get out a clean, white sheet from de bureau. Poor Denis, he couldn'a take it, so dey put him out de room."

"What they used as an anesthetic?" I asked Nanny.

"Anesthetic? Chile yoh mother was in so much pain... a bit more wouldn'a make no difference. An' to besides dey din have much choice." Nanny moved to the side of the road pulling me with her, to allow another car to pass by.

"Anyway... Mama Burke tell me dat Papa cut open Rebecca tummy and bring out de baby. De chile was strong an' healthy as an ox but poor Rebecca bleed so much... she get so weak... dey get real frighten. But she give a weak little smile when dey call Denis in de room an' he look at you an' all he could say is "What a cute little bunnyface she have."

That part of the story, I'd heard many times before. It was the reason for my silly name Boniface. Now that I'd heard the entire story I could more fully appreciate its significance.

By morning time the hurricane had spent itself. When Nanny and Uncle Nat looked outside they couldn't believe the sight that awaited them. It looked as though a dragon breathing fire had passed by. There was not a single leaf on a single tree. You could see for miles around. Several houses were down. Many trees had toppled over including Nanny's large French cashew tree and many breadfruit and mango trees. All banana trees were down. The fowl coup had been crushed by a falling breadfruit tree and all the fowls were gone - many were found dead. Dead animals, fallen coconuts and sheets of galvanized roofing were scattered here and there on the ground.

Foremost on Nanny's mind was Rebecca. The telephone lines were down, so going to the post office to make a phone call was out of the question. That morning Nanny decided she was going to St. George's to see Rebecca.

"But no buses runnin', Mama" said Uncle Nat who had just been talking to a group of neighbours. He'd heard that the main road in many places was blocked by mud slides or huge fallen trees.

"But I ha' to go" Nanny insisted. "Rebecca need me wid her."

Nothing anyone said could have stopped Nanny. She was overcome with a feeling that she needed to be with Rebecca. Uncle Nat and Uncle Benny who came from the adjoining parish to see how his mother and family fared, discovered just how stubborn their mother could be. She was going and that was all there was to it.

"Benny...maybe you should go with Mama," Uncle Nat suggested.

"Don' be silly Nat. Benny ha' to stay wid Theresa an' de baby. Ah gwine be all right."

"But Mama, it gwine take you days to get to St. George's. Where you gwine sleep?"

"Don' worry. When I reach in St. David's I could stay wid me friend Dorothy. Listen nuh... I know lots o' people on de way dat I could stay wid," Nanny lied. She was heartened by the interest of her two youngest sons. Her first son, Dawson, had left home many years ago. He never visited and seldom contacted his mother. She heard he'd gone to England some years ago.

There were many people on the road walking to see how their family in other parts of the island fared. Many injuries and several deaths resulted from this vicious hurricane. Nanny spent the first night with a relative of someone she met on the road. She was still in pretty good shape at that time. The second night she was much more exhausted. Her feet were beginning to give her trouble. The group had thinned out considerably by then. Thankfully someone in the group knew a lady called Hilda Thorne that they could stay with.

They found her easily. She lived up a hill from the main road with her darling little eight-year-old granddaughter, Jessica. Hilda fed all five of the travelers while they discussed their experiences of the hurricane night and the situation of the roads. In the Good Hope area a huge section of the road had sunk forcing everyone to make a long detour through a dark patch of cocoa. Sometimes they had to climb over big trees that had fallen over the road. Hilda still hadn't had any word from her sister and nephew who lived in Gauvine and she was getting anxious. Later she spread out bedding on the floor for the travelers to sleep on.

"You look so tired," she said to Nanny after Nanny had washed up in the back yard, using water as sparingly as possible, since the taps were dry. "Come take the bed in here." She directed Nanny into her bedroom. Nanny would never forget the kindness of this good woman.

A picture on the dresser caught Nanny's attention as she was about to get into bed. It was the picture of a couple - one of whom was her son Dawson.

"What Dawson picture doin' here?" she asked Hilda who was returning to the room.

"You know him?" Hilda asked surprised.

"He me first son"

"Yoh jokin'!"

"An' who she?" Nanny pointed to the woman in the picture.

"Dat is me sister, Mattie."

They both looked at each other in total amazement and smiled. It was as though some invisible force had connected them. What a small world it was, they both agreed.

The next morning, after breakfast, Hilda arranged for a bus to take the travelers as far as possible on the way to St. George's. This was a huge help. Later that morning Nanny knocked on the door of Papa and Mama Burke in Cockroach alley, St. George's.

Denis answered the door. He looked at Nanny like he was seeing a ghost.

"Mama ... dat you?"

"Of course is me. Move leh me come in nuh... how Rebecca?"

"But Mama... how you get here?" Denis was still looking at Nanny in disbelief. "Dey say de roads all block up ..."

Nanny turned around to see Mama and Papa Burke staring at her.

"Good mornin'" Nanny said loudly. "But how come all you watchin' me so? Like I's some jumbie?"

Rebecca had been getting weaker and weaker. Mama Burke was busy taking care of Rebecca. Since there was no water in the taps and no electricity this was no easy task. Luckily Denis was able to get water at a place called Saltfish Hall not too far away. He made a little make shift bed out of a cardboard box for the baby. His mother was feeding her a little sugar water and Denis wondered if that was sufficient for the baby. She seemed to be losing weight. Papa Burke rolled up his sleeves and helped as much as possible. He washed and carefully sterilized all the dirty linens from Rebecca and the baby.

The hospital was so busy with patients injured during the hurricane that volunteers were being solicited for help. A boatload of injured people had arrived from the sister island of Cariacou that morning. Although Mama Burke had asked for a doctor to pay Rebecca a visit, they knew it would take a very long time.

Rebecca was so exhausted she slept a lot. Whenever she was awake she would ask for her mother. Denis explained to her that the roads were blocked and that it would be weeks before they would be fixed.

Transportation had stopped. The telephone lines were also down so they couldn't even get a phone call through to her mother. Rebecca became more and more despondent. All Papa and Mama Burke could think to do was pray.

"Come Denis... let's ask God for help," said Papa Burke. Denis took the baby from her little make shift bed on the table and put her on the bed between himself and Rebecca. He held hands with his mother and father, encircling Rebecca and the baby and prayed for help. Silently Rebecca prayed too. She asked God to send her mother to her.

Suddenly there was a loud knocking at the door. Denis gave the baby to Mama Burke and went to answer the door.

Nanny got the shock of her life when she saw Rebecca, who looked one step away from death's door. The smell of death hung in the room, she said. Although small, the baby was still strong - she had a robust cry but poor Rebecca was in a bad way.

"Mama?" Rebecca whispered as Nanny entered the room. "I know you were comin' Mama."
Nanny bent down and kissed Rebecca on the cheek.

Rebecca improved gradually. Nanny remained with her at all times while Mama Burke took care of the baby and did the cooking. Papa Burke continued to help with the washing and sterilizing and Denis made sure there was sufficient water and food in the house.

"Everybody chip in an' help," said Nanny. "An' by de end of de nex' week Rebecca take ah turn for de

better. She start sittin' up in bed laughin' an' playin' wid de baby."
Nanny placed her arm around my shoulder. We had reached the top of the gap leading down to her home. "So you see, de Lord sho is good. Never forget to praise God. Look you now nuh. A fine young lady about to go 'way."
I placed my arm around her thick waist. I felt I had just relived an important part of history - my history.

8

I was in two minds about whether to attend the dinner at Herbert and Adlyn's home. I felt both Regina and Ad were trying to set me up with Todd and I resisted that. The insinuation that I was so lacking in charm or whatever it takes to hook my own 'prey', did not gratify me in the least. On the other hand I could kick back and enjoy some excellent food and great company. Ad had also invited Jessica and Curt Lincoln, who were visiting from Toronto and Madge and Willie Johnson with their daughter Ayanna, who was Tiffany's age. I'd met the Johnsons once before and it would be a pleasure to meet them again. Both Jessica and Madge were 'home folks'. So when Ad called to say that 'Erbie' was going to pick me up at six o' clock, I didn't concoct an excuse.

I almost didn't recognize Herbie whom I noticed immediately was minus the usual scruffy hat, which had become an extension of him. Regardless of the season, Herbie wore his sweat stained fedora. He even seemed to have shaved and I liked that striped shirt and light coloured pants he was wearing. Without a doubt superhuman efforts by Ad were responsible for this get up.

Herbie and I pulled into their driveway at their south Ottawa home at six thirty. Regina and Tiffany were already there. Regina was at the kitchen sink, helping Ad with something while Tiffany was lying on the carpeted floor of the living room stuffing herself with nuts and chips. Mouthwatering smells exuded from the kitchen reminding me of how starved I was. Calypso music was blasting from the stereo as Ad dressed in a beautiful and colourful caftan sang along loudly.

Drunk and disorderly
Tatata tata tata
Drunk and disorderly
Tatata tata tata.

"Hi Boni!" Ad interrupted her singing to greet me and deposited a loud smack on my cheek. "Erbie ... you check de ice yet?" Then back to me. "So how you doin', darlin'?" As I was about to answer, the doorbell rang and she hurried to answer it.

Regina and I exchanged greetings. She wore her hair all slicked down to her head in finger waves, setting off her eyes and cheekbones beautifully. I joined Tiffany in the living room sitting next to a table laden with little porcelain figurines. Adlyn was the queen of trinkets. It was no use trying to pretend I could be useful in Ad's kitchen and offer any help. Besides Herbie was every bit as proficient as Ad in that department. I hoped Regina wasn't messing up anything.

"Hi Aunt Boni" said Tiffany.

"Hi darling" I responded as I hugged Tiffany. "You got back your Nightingale project yet?"

"Not yet" Tiffany replied as a cute, young girl about Tiffany's age sauntered down the hallway to the living room. That must be Ayanna Johnson, I thought. She and Tiffany greeted each other, then she looked up at me.

"Hello... I'm Ayanna," she said to me quite formally as she held out her hand. She was quite the little lady.

Then came her parents, Madge and Willie, and behind them a tall, nutmeg-coloured, gorgeous woman whom I assumed was Jessica Lincoln with her husband Curtis a few steps behind her. We all greeted each other as Ad and Herbie made the necessary introductions.

"Is only Todd to come now," Adlyn announced, "but in the meantime what y'all drinking?" Then before anyone could answer. "Erbie fix dem a drink nuh. Don' mek dem die wid thirst man." We all chuckled at Ad's humour.

"I gwine fix de ladies" said Herbert smiling. "But fellers come and pour yoh own poison."

Todd was already almost an hour late. I could tell Adlyn was beginning to get ticked off. After all he was the catalyst that had sparked this dinner party. But while we waited we got reacquainted with one another and enjoyed the hors d'oeuvres which were so tasty, I had to remind myself not to spoil my dinner by having too many.

"Teaching is getting more and more difficult each year," Willie Johnson declared. He was a teacher at Forrest Stetson high school.

"Why? What's the cause of that?" I wanted to know.

"It's a multitude of factors... more and more difficult children... but most of all parents not doing their jobs."

"And what's that?" asked Regina.

"Parenting," replied Willie simply.

Regina squirmed. She looked over at Tiffany whom we could see in the family room playing a computer game with Ayanna. "I agree," she said softly. "Some parents just let their kids run wild all over the place. It makes it much more difficult for other parents like me."

I remembered my resolve to talk to Regina about letting Tiffany go to the mall if she did well on her Nightingale project. I hadn't had the opportunity to bring it up yet. Every time I called her she was just about to go out. I gathered there was a new gentleman on the horizon.

Madge looked over at Regina sympathetically. "I know how you feel but on the other hand you can't keep them locked up. You have to let go of the reins bit by bit."

My point exactly. I smiled at Madge.

"You'd be surprised to know what some of these kids are in to, and you'd hate for your child to be among them," said Regina animatedly, looking in my direction for support but finding none. I didn't think Tiffany should be penalized for the actions of others. She turned to Jessica, who was sitting with her legs elegantly crossed. Curt was just handing her a drink he'd mixed for her. He was the most attentive husband I'd seen in a long time. "What do you think Jess?"

"There's a lot of peer pressure influence it's true but you can't watch your child 24/7," said Jessica. The array of silver bracelets on her arm chimed lightly as she accepted her drink from Curt.

"Sooner or later they're going to flee the nest," added Curt. "So you'd better make sure your influence is in the mix and it's the best and the strongest."

"Then what?" asked Adlyn, who was just returning from the kitchen. Of the group, she and I were the only women without children although Herbie's daughter and Adlyn's stepdaughter, Sharon, often spent time with her and Herbie.

Curt decided to answer. "If you still need to watch their every move, that's too bad. You hope and pray that by then the values you have taught them ..."

Adlyn butt in. "I think what Reg wants to know is when to start letting go of the reins." She looked over at Regina who nodded.

"It varies with different children," suggested Jessica. "I believe in starting slowly, then depending on results giving more or pulling back a bit."

I nodded in agreement as I looked at Regina. There was still a question mark on her face.

"What if you hear that some of their friends are into stuff," said Regina, with a flailing of her right hand.

Willie who had remained silent for a while, put his glass down to answer Regina. "I think parents must step up to the plate. They have to give their children boundaries."

"But you can't lock them up" interjected Madge. I got the feeling that this was a running debate with them.

Willie continued. "Parents should know at all times where their children are, whom they're with and what they're doing." He enumerated on his fingers as he quietly made his point. He was a tall, skinny guy while his wife, Madge, was short and pleasantly plump with dimpled cheeks. They reminded me of a couple in Grenada nicknamed Pin and Cushion because of those same physical attributes.

Regina shook her head. "If you're a single parent that's impossible," she said.

Todd burst into the room like a strong gust of wind. He carried a mixed bouquet of flowers "for the beautiful ladies" he announced, without making any apologies for being late. He handed the bouquet to Adlyn to put in a vase. "BeeBee... that red rose in the middle is for you," he said loudly, succeeding in making me turn as red as the rose, as all eyes looked from Todd to me. With his booming voice the noise level had definitely stepped up a decibel.

"Now that Todd's finally here...let's go straight to the dining room," said Herbert.

"Hey man... nuttin' to wet de throat first?" Todd asked Herbie, feigning amazement.

"At the table man... we starvin'."

There was a beautiful spread in the dining room. Somehow this couple combined hearty, wholesome delicious food with a magnificent setting. The china complemented the cheerful colours of the tablecloth and dinner napkins.

"Beautiful" said Jessica and Madge together.

Ad gushed with pride.

The meal was definitely a hit with Todd. It was surely different from the one he had in my apartment yesterday. "Like I always say Herbie," he remarked as he helped himself to more escovitched fish - I think it was his third helping - "you should open a restaurant."

The look on Adlyn's face told me that Todd had hit on something that she or maybe both of them had been thinking about. "Yeah man," continued Todd. "Nobody do this thing like you."

Herbert worked as a repair/delivery man for a refrigeration company. He was extremely good with his hands but having never had much formal education, a lot of doors remained closed to him.

Ad changed the subject as she looked at Jessica. "But you never say how de twins dem doing."

Jessica smiled. "They're doing fine" she said. "Jolene is now in law school and Josh is doing his MBA." Josh and Jolene were the twins Jessica had when she was still a teenager. I gathered she'd come to Canada and then sent for them to join her and Curt, whom she had recently married.

"You makin' joke" Ad remarked. "Already?"

"Fantastic," I said. "You must be very proud of them."

"We are" answered Jessica. Ting a' ling went her decorated right arm as gesturing at Curt, Madge and Willie, she continued. "All these guys here had a hand in it...they all helped to raise them."

"It won't make no difference though," mumbled Todd. His mood had suddenly darkened. Everyone looked at him.

"What?" said Curt.

"No matter how qualified you are, it don't make a difference in the long run."

To my surprise, Curt nodded. "To some extent you have a point" he said. Then after a while added, "I agree with you...there is this quality called *The Fit* which is totally subjective..."

"And you think that's fair," retorted Todd.

"No" said Curt. "But once you know the game, you learn to play it."

"Play the game?" said Madge, "The problem is when you go to apply for a job and *The Fit* carries more weight than the other requirements for the position."

"I think it does more often than we know," Curt concluded.

"When *The Fit* means you have to be a certain prescribed way, have qualities that have nothing to do with performance, how can you play the game?" I asked Curt.

"That's right," said Madge. She was right in there with me. "What if *The Fit* requires you to look or sound a certain way and that has nothing to do with job performance?" She underlined my point.

Curt cleared his throat. He was about to answer when Jessica jumped in. "Josh went for an interview some months ago," she said "and the interviewer spent most of the time talking about soccer and football with him."

"He never asked Josh a single technical question relating to the job," continued Curt.

Todd shook his head. I could tell that for him this was a very sore subject. Happily Ayanna changed the topic by accidentally spilling some gravy on her dress.

"Oh Oh!" she exclaimed. She was quite upset. Madge wiped the spill with a napkin and then they both excused themselves from the table and went to the bathroom to clean it up better.

When they returned the conversation drifted to what Ayanna and Tiffany were up to. I wasn't surprised to hear that Ayanna - so slim and petite - was into gymnastics. Tiffany looked uncomfortable when it was her turn to say what she was doing. According to Regina all Tiffany desired was to hang out with friends. I came to her aid. "Tiffany loves to read," I said. "And do you know she just completed a great project on Florence Nightingale?" Tiffany beamed with pride as she went on to describe her discovery of how Nightingale related to Mary Secole. Everyone was visibly impressed with the level of her research.

"Tiffany... that's great," said Willie.

I knew she was thrilled when Madge invited her to come over to their home to visit with Ayanna sometimes.

"And what about Sharon?" said Jessica to both Ad and Herbie as she helped herself and Curt to more chicken. Ad shook her head. That was a sensitive subject. At twenty, not only had she never worked a single day in her life but according to Ad, Sharon had been displaying the morals of an alley cat. "She need some good discipline in her backside," Ad had said to me. Her mother didn't want her doing any 'crappy' menial jobs - a point of view Ad totally disagreed with. "It would build character," she'd insisted and I had agreed with her. I also knew Herbert was paying both child support and alimony - 'all de money' as Ad put it - to his ex wife, which was also a sore topic with Adlyn. But leave it to Ad, as in a cheery voice she replied to Jessica, "Sharon still Sharon," then recalled the old back-home adage "One day, one day, congotay." Everyone chuckled.

The conversation settled for a while on sports, especially cricket. Todd reverted to his old guffawing self again. By the time dessert was served everyone was listening intently to Herbie's manicou hunting escapades. He reminded me of my Uncle Nat.

"They live in tree holes," said Herbie.

"So how you know when a manicou's in the hole?" asked Curt. He was born in Montreal, so stories like this were new to him.

"You jus' push a stick up de hole man an if when you pull it out, you see bits of fur on it... you know one in dey."

"What?" Ayanna and Tiffany were listening intently. "And what if it's home?"

Herbert laughed. He was enjoying telling this story.

"If it home you gwine hear a soft growling sound," answered Herbie.

"So what next?" asked Regina.

Todd interjected. "Don't tell me you push up yoh hand, man."

"Of course," said Herbie.

"But dey have razor sharp teeth," Willie pointed out.

"Yeah...Yeah" agreed Herbie. "But manicou always stay in de tree wid de tail hanging down an' de head up."

"Dat so?" Curt was impressed.

"So all you have to do is wrap de tail 'round yoh hand quick, quick." Herbie stood up to demonstrate. Ayanna winced, bringing her shoulders up to her ears. "Then you pull it down fast an' wid one quick motion bash de head real hard on de tree before it turn 'round an' bite yoh." Herbie demonstrated how this was done.

"You kill it?" Tiffany didn't think this was funny. I wondered what she thought had been done to the chicken she'd just eaten. I had a feeling she thought of chicken as something frozen in the supermarket and not as a live bird hopping around. Like most children born in North American cities, she could do with a dose of reality.

I decided to entertain the group with a story of my cousin Henry nicknamed Stonehead. When he was a little boy, he climbed a mango tree and stuffed himself silly with all the ripe, half-ripe and 'bird-jook' fruit within reach. Finally as he was about to come down, he saw a beautiful orange and yellow mango off to his right. Although full, he decided he couldn't leave such a perfect mango behind. But as he leaned forward and stretched out his hand to pick this lovely mango, it slowly began to uncoil. It was a serpent! Releasing the branch that supported him, Stonehead fell twenty feet to the ground below, screaming like the dickens.

"Serpents can camouflage themselves real well," said Todd as he laughed heartily.

"Did he hurt himself?" Madge wanted to know.

"No... luckily the branches of the tree broke his fall sufficiently."

"Aunt Boni... I want to go with you to Grenada next time you visit," said Tiffany with an earnest look in her eyes.

"I was there last year," Ayanna recalled proudly. "Mum and Dad took me there on a holiday."

I looked over at Regina, who had come to this country with her mother from Guyana when she was only five years old. Her mother later passed away and Regina had never returned to the place of her birth, so it seemed all ties had been severed.

"Sure," I replied to Tiffany. "If your Mum agrees."

9

Todd insisted on driving me home after the dinner at Ad and Herbie's. I assumed Regina was going to take me home but she claimed she had another stop to make and was running late. I suspected this was all part of the big set up.

"Here...don't forget your rose." Adlyn handed me the red rose Todd had said was for me, as I exited the front door.

I yawned a couple times in the car to disabuse Todd of any notion that he was coming up to my apartment with me. It was long after midnight and my bed beckoned.

"I guess you don't feel like going to a bar," he said.

"Bar! I've already had more than enough to drink tonight," I answered. "And they're all probably closing in a few minutes." I don't know why I added that - I guess I wanted to refuse him gently.

"I'm going back to Toronto tomorrow... and I was hoping to spend time with you before I leave."

I didn't answer. Didn't we spend time together yesterday? We got to my apartment building and Todd swung to the left presumably to check out the 'visitor parking', which thankfully was full. He continued around the circle and stopped just before the front entrance of the building.

"Thanks so much for bringing me home Todd," I said. "And thanks for this." I added, gesturing at the lone rose.

Todd winced. "Not even a little kiss BeeBee?"
I blew a kiss in his direction as I opened the car door. "There" I said as my feet hit the pavement. "Now have a safe drive back to Toronto tomorrow."

"I'm a patient man BeeBee... I can wait" he said, smiling.

I walked swiftly towards the front door, then turned around. Just as I thought - his eyes were glued to my behind. At age thirty seven, the whole world seemed to conspire to warn me that my biological clock was not just ticking but banging loudly - ding dong, ding dong. Unfair, since at this point most brothers are considered at the peak of eligibility. So who was I to be so picky? I must admit that sometimes I felt that although the man for me had not yet been born, his mother was surely dead. I waved at Todd's grinning face as the door to the building slammed behind me.

Adlyn agreed to go to the car dealership with me to check out the new *Firefly* models that I fancied. At the close of work yesterday Mason told me that his uncle had purchased the same model I was interested in from *Henry's* dealership. It was a graduation gift for his daughter. He gave me the specs as well as the price his uncle had paid for it.

"*C'est très belle!*" exclaimed Mason. "Go girl go" he said, as he grabbed me by the hands and pirouetted around the empty unit. Mason was planning to move to the west coast within the coming year and although it might mean a chance of promotion for me, I was going to miss him and his clownish ways extremely.

I was very excited. Regina was busy and couldn't come too, which in a way suited me fine because Regina has been known to make the worse financial decisions in history. But Ad was free and yes, she had a lot more business savvy than Reg. Not to mention she was curious to find out how things went with Todd and me last Saturday night.

"I have nothing juicy to report," I told her as she gave me the unbelieving eye.

"You know de man come all de way here because o' you?" Ad was looking at me accusingly.

"So?"

"Him tell Erbie you de first woman in a long time dat really turn him on," Ad said as she giggled.

"I'm just getting to know him," I said. "I believe in going very slowly with relationships." I stressed the 'very slowly'.

Ad rolled her eyes at me. "Yoh gettin' on like you still sixteen." I knew that was a comment on my ticking biological clock.

We sat across a table from a suited, smiling *Henry's* salesman, who introduced himself as Jake. While we were looking at brochures of the Mark II models of the

Firefly, Jake wondered whether we'd like something to drink.

"Certainly" said Ad, before I could refuse. I was too nervous to drink anything. Buying a new car was not something I did everyday. "What do you have?"

"Coffee? Or something cold maybe?"

"Definitely something cold" replied Ad, answering for me again, this time smiling at the salesman.

"Okay...okay" said Jake. "Some pop or..."

"Or..." said Ad prompting him along.

"Wine? Would you like some wine?"

"That would be just fine," replied Ad. "We would like some wine."

Then as Jake left to fetch the wine, she whispered to me, "You gwine be payin' for all dis shit, so you might as well drink up."

"Be serious" I chided Ad as I poured over some brochures before me. I asked her to come along with me to help me - not for dramatic entertainment.

Jake returned with the wine.

"So Jake" I said to him, pointing at the model on the table in front of me. I had scribbled down all the specs that I wanted him to include. "What is the best price you can give me on this one?"

Jake went into the back room to talk with his manager and after a few minutes came back to our table smiling.

"You're in luck," he said. "We have a model here now and if you take it we can make you an excellent price."

My heart sang with joy. "Wow! That's great," I said. I could hardly hide my excitement. I took the brochure from Jake's extended right arm. I went down the list of specs on this vehicle. There was no air conditioning which was on my list of 'must haves.'

"So what's your price?" I asked, looking up at him.

Jake gave me what he said was his best price. I couldn't believe my ears. I began to laugh. It was way higher than what Mason's uncle had paid for his daughter's vehicle, which not only had air conditioning but was specially ordered for her. He didn't take any damned car from the lot either.

"You're kidding me," I said.

"That's your best price?" asked Adlyn as she sipped her wine.

Jake looked rather frazzled for a while. "I guess I should tell you that we can finance the whole deal for you. We have a financial package that is..."

I put my hand up. I knew he wanted to start a whole lot of financial gobbledygook to snow me over with. "Please" I said. "Just give me your very best price for a vehicle with the specs that I have given you."

"So you don't want this one?" he asked referring to the model in the lot that he was trying to push. I was getting a bit impatient.

"Does it have all the specs on this list here?"

"It has much more than what's on your list," said Jake. "Tinted glass, burglar alarm and radial tires...it's only the air conditioning it doesn't..."

"That's right," said Ad looking directly at Jake and speaking slowly. "No air conditioning...no sell." I think Ad saw this as an interesting game that she was prepared to enjoy to the hilt.

Jake scratched his head and retreated once more to the back room. When he returned, he placed before me a brochure of a car with the specs that I had initially requested.

"Good," I replied after going down the list. Then I handed it back to him. "Now give me the very best price that you can on this model."

Jake pushed numbers on his calculator for a few minutes then with a sullen face, scribbled the price on the brochure. "I won't be making much commission on this deal," he muttered.

I looked at what he'd written. Still way above what Mason's uncle had paid.

"Sorry but I'm definitely not happy with this price and if that's the best you can do, then we can't do business." I picked up my purse from the floor beside me and started getting up from my chair.

"Okay...okay...wait a second," said Jake and disappeared to the back room again. I sat back down.

"Yoh squeezin' 'im right in 'im crotch" said Adlyn giggling underneath her breath.

Jake returned with an older guy, meticulously groomed and dressed in what looked like a very expensive suit. He smiled benevolently at us.

"You don't have to worry about a thing, girls," he said. That reference to us as 'girls' galled me. "We can finance the whole deal for you. You can get your car without putting down a cent." He opened his eyes widely as if to imply who would have thought such a miracle was possible.

I said nothing. I simply tapped the table with my fingers, as I looked up at Jake, who was standing right behind Miracle Man. Ad smiled sweetly up at this good gentleman and took another sip of wine - my wine.

When we left the dealership that evening, I had an even better deal than Mason's uncle. What made it sweeter and cost me less is the fact that I did not need to take advantage of their miracle financial package with its whopping 18% interest rate. I was pleased with myself. I had done my research and it had certainly paid off.

"Mek we go have a drink an' celebrate" said Ad as she drove me home afterwards.

"You drunk already," I teased her, reminding her of my wine that she had 'downed' at the dealership.

I called Regina the next day to tell her the good news about my new car. She wasn't home and Tiffany answered the phone.

"Hi darling... what's happening?"

"Nothing" she answered. I could tell from the tone of her voice that something was not quite right.

"What's the matter?" I asked. I definitely heard a sniff.

"Nothing" she insisted.

"Is Mum at home?"

"No... she left a message saying she was going to be late." Another little sniff. This time it was undeniable. Usually when Regina worked late, she had Tiffany stay with me or occasionally with Adlyn. She never liked leaving Tiffany for long periods by herself. This was a switch. Something was wrong. I wasn't sure what it was but I could feel it.

"Okay... I'm coming right over," I said at the spur of the moment.

Tiffany let me into their 10th floor apartment and I could tell from her red eyes that she was upset and had been crying.

"Hi Tiff," I said as I hugged her. I thought I'd give her a chance to tell me what was bothering her without my prying. I noticed the TV was on, which I knew was an absolute no-no on Regina's list of rules. Until all homework was done, there was to be no TV. "You're finished your homework already?"

Tiffany pouted. "No" she said defiantly. "And I'm not doing any." With that she stomped off to her bedroom, loudly slamming the door shut behind her. I was taken aback. I thought I'd leave her for a while to let off steam. After a few minutes I knocked at her bedroom door. She didn't answer. I opened the door slowly and peeped in. Tiffany was lying face down on her bed sobbing.

"What's the matter Tiff?" I sat on her bed and gently rubbed her back. She didn't answer. Her school bag had been thrown on the floor and half its contents were spilling out of it. Something caught my eye and as I pulled at it, I noticed it was the Nightingale project that she had gotten back.

"My God!" I said in total amazement as I looked at the project. I couldn't believe this teacher. All references to Mary Secole had been viciously crossed out with a red marker and the word "Irrelevant" written in the margins. Tiffany received 51% for this assignment that had no spelling errors, no grammatical errors and all her facts had been carefully researched and referenced. Something was definitely wrong here. I looked at Tiffany who was now sitting on the bed and looking in my direction. I felt a flood of sympathy for her. This poor child came home from school hurting deeply, only to find a note from her mother that she was going to be late. I was getting suspicious of Regina and all this 'work' she was doing recently.

"Tiffany," I said, pulling her to me. "We are going to talk to your teacher about this project."

"It's no use," Tiffany whimpered. "It won't make any difference."

"Of course it will," I said, thinking that my university major in English must surely be worth something. "Mum and I are going to pay Mrs. Howard a visit and find out what the problems are."

"Mum won't have any time," Tiffany responded.

"She'll make time...this is important."

Tiffany wiped her nose. I could tell she appreciated having someone backing her.

"That was the lowest mark in the class," said Tiffany.

I was stunned. It would be nice if I could get hold of a real bad project that received a better mark, to add clout when we met that Mrs. Howard. As I was contemplating the best way to do so Tiffany said,

"Even Andrew John got a better mark than me. He got 55%."

My plan was formed. I asked Tiffany to borrow Andrew's project as well as Sylvia's - the girl who received the highest mark in the class and bring them to me. We weren't going to take this sitting down. She was to let Andrew and Sylvia believe she simply wanted to compare projects to see her downfall.

Regina came in around midnight and was stunned to see me half asleep on her couch.

"What happen Boni?... Tiffany okay?"

"Hi Reg. I came over to keep Tiffany company when she told me you were working late." Regina was carrying a bouquet of roses. "I see you picked up some lovely roses...eh?"

"Thanks... but you didn't have to," she said ignoring my last comment.

"No? I thought you didn't like her staying by herself for such long periods." I looked at my watch deliberately.

"Well you know... she's growing up... I have to start easing her in slowly."

I thought to myself that this was like dumping her into the deep end. It wasn't a slow start at all. However before I called a taxi to take me home, I got to the main point. "Tiffany got back her Nightingale project today. She's very upset. She got 51% which was the lowest mark in the class."

A frown concentrated on Regina's forehead. I continued. "I think you should definitely make an appointment to see Mrs. Howard and I'm willing to come along with you."

"What? When am I going to do that?"

"Can you call Mrs. Howard tomorrow and make an appointment?"

"I can't be running to the school every time Tiffany screws up... I have to earn a living you know."

"Tiffany didn't screw up. There is something wrong... and as her mother you should find out." I looked Regina straight in the eye. "Like I said, I will take a couple hours off work to come with you."

"You know Boni... Tiffany is *my* responsibility not yours." Was she telling me to butt out? She had some nerve. I picked up the phone and dialed *Rightaway* taxi service. I gathered my things and headed for the door.

"Good bye" I said curtly. If Regina thought I was done with her she was sadly mistaken. But I knew the walls of this apartment were paper-thin and just in case Tiffany was awake, I didn't want her to hear us arguing. But I was definitely going to get back to Regina with a piece of my mind.

10

There were six calls on my answering machine when I checked my voice messages upon my return home from work, after stopping off at the supermarket. I'd taken a taxi home since I'd picked up more items than I'd planned to. The fruit looked so tempting I couldn't stop myself and I was all out of those bulky items like toilet paper and paper towel.

The first call said "Aunt Boni... I have Andrew John's and Sylvia's assignments. Okay?" The next call was also from Tiffany. "Aunt Boni, Mum just called me. She said she has to go out of town for a week and I'm going to be staying with Aunt Ad. Please... can I stay with you instead Aunt Boni?" Of course she can stay with me, but why did Regina not call me? The third was from Jake at the car dealership confirming the time when I could pick up my car. "Boni give me a call when you get this message okay?" Adlyn's high-pitched voice said "and tell me nuh... what goin' on wid you and Reg?" The fifth caller cheerfully announced that I had won a vacation trip to somewhere. All I had to do was call... "Leave me alone," I said irritably as I promptly engaged the delete button. Finally the sixth caller said "BeeBee is me. I'll call back later."

"Wo-o-oy" I spoke loudly to myself. "This place is like Grand Central." Anyhow, first things first. I called Tiffany.

"Hello," Tiffany's voice answered.

I thought I'd go right away and pick up the projects before Regina got home. She was obviously a little pissed with me and let's face it, the feeling was reciprocated. "Hi Tiffany, I got your calls. Of course you can stay with me next week, darling."

"Thanks Aunt Boni... I thought so. I'll tell Mum."

"And I'm coming over in a short while to get the projects."

"It's okay Aunt Boni... you... you don't have to. I... I... I'm doing my homework now Aunt Boni." There was a distinct and unfamiliar stutter in her voice. Did I hear muted voices in the background?

"Tiffany, is your Mum home?"

"No... Mum's working late tonight." That's what I thought. This 'working late' was becoming the norm.

"Who's there Tiffany?"

"Whaaat? Nobody's here Aunt Boni," Tiffany insisted. I knew that was a lie.

"Okay then... I'll be over shortly." I hung up the receiver before she could get another word in and immediately dialed *Rightaway*. At this rate I should own shares in that taxi company. My new car was coming not a minute too soon, it seems. I'll talk to Ad later. But this was urgent. Regina had gone from one extreme to the other. First she wouldn't let Tiffany stay one minute by herself, now the child was being left alone for hours on end - sometimes way into the night. God knows what kind of mischief she was getting into.

 Someone held the door open for me as I got to the Southpark apartment building, so I didn't have to buzz Tiffany to let me in. The elevator was right there too. What luck! I got out of the elevator on the 10th floor and headed down the hallway to apartment 1004. Before I could get there, the door was flung open and a young boy with a red baseball cap, and pants slipping off his behind, followed a grumpy, young, mini-skirted girl, balancing a cigarette between her lips, out the door.

 "Don't think we'll ever f---ing come back here Tiffany," the young girl was saying annoyed. "that's just not f---ing cool."

 "Yea... It f---ing sucks" said the young boy.

 "You don't understand," I heard Tiffany pleading. "My aunt's coming over any minute now. I tried but I just couldn't stop..." Tiffany's bewildered eyes were now staring straight into my face.

I walked back to my apartment after my short visit with Tiffany. I felt I needed the exercise as much as I needed to clear my head. Yesterday Regina had distinctly told me that Tiffany was her responsibility and not mine. But she was a child in crisis. What should I do?

 After the scene at the door, where I had literally 'busted' her, Tiffany had hung her head in guilt and shame. I had asked her for the assignments she'd gotten for me and she had handed them over meekly.

 "Were those your friends?" I inquired in a soft voice referring to the vile mouth youths I had encountered at the door.

"They're in my class," she answered. I wondered whether their assignments for Mrs. Howard were laced with as many expletives as they spoke.

"Does Mum know they visit you here?" I asked.

"No" answered Tiffany. "This is the first time they came here." Tears rolled down her cheek. "Please don't tell Mum about this Aunt Boni," and before I responded, added "I promise I won't do it again and I won't lie to you again either."

"Tiffany," I said. "I'm willing to help you. But I have to be able to trust you."

"I know Aunt Boni" she replied tearfully.

The phone was ringing as I entered my apartment.

"Where you been to, gal?" asked Ad. "So long me trying to reach you."

"Out walking... why... what's the matter?"

"Well two t'ings. Regina want me keep Tiffany for her next week. She say she have to go 'way and you too busy for Tiffany stay wid you."

"What a bunch of crap," I blurted out. "She never asked me." Ever since I had met Regina, I had been baby-sitting Tiffany for her all the time. I have become a sort of surrogate aunt to Tiffany. Ad filled in occasionally but only when I wasn't available.

"Y'all have a fight or somet'ing?" Ad asked.

I didn't want to get into that business with Ad. I simply said "If Regina wants I can baby-sit her daughter next week."

"Me t'ought so," answered Adlyn.

"And where is Miss Lady off to?" I asked.

"Vegas, me dear... an' dat's de next t'ing me want talk to you 'bout."

"Ehheh?" I said to Adlyn. "Is this business or pleasure?"

"How it could be business?"

"What's going on Ad?"

"Me no know, me dear, but lately she spendin' money like water. You know she jus' buy a brand new living room set and new TV?"

"Eh?"

"She ask Erbie to go over to her apartment nex' week when dey deliverin' her stuff."

"That so?"

"Since she start goin' wid dis new man, Regina like she losin' it. Me bet is him she goin' to Vegas wid. You know Erbie friend see dem in de casino over in Hull late, late last night."

I sighed. "Poor Tiffany" I said. I couldn't believe my ears. Regina had no time for an appointment with Mrs. Howard about Tiffany's English project but she had all the time in the world for casinos and Vegas and the like. I was rip roaring mad now.

I called Mother at home in Grenada. A juvenile little voice answered the phone. I knew it had to be one of Uncle Nat's many grandchildren. His daughter Patty, nicknamed MLP, and her brood of children lived close to Mother and were in and out of the house all the time.

"How you doin' Bunnyface?" Mother asked when she took the phone. She was the only person on this earth who still called me that.

"Fine Mother. I was speaking to Brenda about y'all coming up to visit next year."

"Yea?... dat is Brenda's idea... but I..."

"Mother, it's fine. I'm looking forward to it."

"But you have space for us nuh?"
"By then I will Mother.. don't worry."
"What... you changin' apartments?"
"Mother... I didn't tell you but I'm planning to buy a little townhouse." I decided to let her in on this plan, which I initially thought I'd keep as a surprise.
"But I don' want you puttin' yourself in any debt, Bunny."
"Don't worry Mother, I won't." Mother and Daddy had always been paranoid about debt. I never understood why, until as an adult I learned how Papa and Mama Burke, who at one time owned quite a lucrative business in Gauvine, lost all their assets by taking a loan from a large proprietor. When on one month they were unable to make the payment, a writ of execution was secured from the court and the proprietor was able to acquire all their assets. Papa Burke was forced to spend many years in Venezuela working to pay off this debt, so that he could at the very minimum get back his home. "It may not be properly furnished by then" I assured her. "But we'll definitely have the space."
"I can't wait to see you again, Bunnyface." I knew Mother was sold on the idea now.
"I can hardly wait myself," I added.

Somehow it didn't surprise me. With two spelling errors, Sylvia got 90% for her Nightingale paper. It was an excellent paper which I used to compare with Tiffany's. Tiffany had included every single point made by Sylvia in her paper. The difference was obviously the reference to Mary Secole. The comparison with Andrew's untidy, sloppy paper was far more dramatic.

It contained less than half of the points that Tiffany and Sylvia included in theirs, and earned him 55%.

I felt compelled to stick my nose out for Tiffany. She would be staying with me next week, when her mother goes to Las Vegas. That would be an excellent time to make an appointment to see Mrs. Howard and if I had to I would see the school principal. After all I would be officially in the role of caretaker. I would introduce myself as Tiffany's aunt and guardian.

Todd had been calling every day this week. When he called tonight, I asked if I could call him right back. Actually I was concerned about his phone bill, knowing he was far from loaded. He was an avid sports follower and could talk for hours about hockey or football or baseball - he even followed cricket matches. I didn't share his passion but made little polite responses.

Tonight he asked when I was coming back to Toronto, carefully suggesting that I shouldn't let the 'incident' of my last visit deter me.

"Not at all" I answered too quickly. "That's totally behind me now."

"Way to go BeeBee," he said. I don't think he believed me one bit. "So how about next weekend then?"

I explained that I was tied up for quite a while. I had a great deal on my plate. I mentioned having to baby sit Tiffany, since Regina had to go out of town.

"Talking about Regina... I been trying to get hold of her... tell her for me her parcel coming next week."

Parcel? Some more purchases? What was that all about I wondered, but I decided to mind my own business.

"Like I said Todd, Regina's going away next week."

"Well she can make arrangements with the janitor to get it for her."

To change the subject, since I was passing on none of this to Regina, I tried to divert the conversation to him. "So Todd... how's your search for a teaching position going?"

His mood changed immediately. "I'm never going back to teaching," he said solemnly.

"You serious?"

"BeeBee... please don't talk to me about teaching again." He slammed the phone down. Amazed, I held the receiver. What was that all about? The curtain had definitely come down.

11

I almost canceled my appointment with Mrs. Howard because by the time I left work I was so emotionally drained. It was one of those times from hell when one has to dig deep just to stay afloat. The clinic was a beehive of activity all morning but thankfully by afternoon it began to slow down.

"I don't know what I'd do without you," Mason complimented me.

I was glad he noticed and I hoped he hadn't forgotten that I had asked to leave work half an hour early today for an important appointment. Well, I won't let him.

I had everything under control until I decided to help Francine with one of her patients. To expedite matters, I put the preservative into the urine bottle before giving it to the patient to take into the bathroom for a sample. When to my surprise, he returned the empty bottle to me, I asked "You didn't leave a sample?" thinking maybe he was bone dry and wasn't able to urinate. But what the patient, who had a limited knowledge of English, responded, sent the blood rushing to my head.

"Jink it," he said as he demonstrated. "I jink it." He had drunk the preservative in the bottle. "Oh my God!" I exclaimed as I called Mason nervously. "Do you know what's in the preservative?"

We didn't wait to call down to the lab to find out - it could be cyanide or some other toxic substance. We hastened to induce vomiting in the patient and of course a doctor was summoned and the perpetual paper work had to be filled out and submitted. I should have ensured that the patient clearly understood what he had to do with a urine bottle. I was relieved that the patient had not been harmed but I was shaken by that experience and the knowledge that this incident report could possibly jeopardize my chances of an upcoming promotion, weighed heavily on my mind.

As I drove west on the highway I felt in no state of mind to confront yet another hurdle - Mrs. Howard. Thick raindrops splattered my windshield decreasing the visibility on the highway and forcing me to reduce my speed. I pulled into the parking lot with three minutes to spare and hastily had someone direct me to Mrs. Howard's office. She noticeably looked at her watch as I entered the room.

"Hello Mrs. Howard," I said with a fake smile. "Am I late?" I consulted my watch as well. I was smack on time.

"Hello Miss Burke," she answered pointing to a chair nearby. She did not answer about the time. "You are here I believe about Tiffany Doyle?" she asked as she peered over her horn-rimmed glasses.

I took the seat offered as I unzipped my briefcase. "Yes Mrs. Howard... I would like to discuss Tiffany's Nightingale project with you."

Beneath the Surface

"What about it?" she said sternly as she folded her arms and sat back in her chair. She was a lanky woman heavily made up, lips glistening with bright pink lipstick. Her entire forehead was covered with thick black, perfectly coifed hair, while ornate jewelry decorated her swan-like neck, earlobes and wrists. I had a feeling she thought she was hot stuff.

"First of all I would like to let you know that Tiffany put a great deal of effort into this assignment and she is quite disappointed with her mark."

"So?"

"So I thought I'd come to find out where her shortcomings were."

"Did I not indicate that on the paper?"

I slipped Tiffany's paper out of my briefcase, leaving behind copies of Sylvia's and Andrew's for the time being. "You mentioned only her reference to Mary Secole, which you thought was irrelevant." I stressed *you* then continued. "Was there anything else?"

Mrs. Howard unfolded her arms and leaned forward in her chair. "She was totally off topic," she said, her blue eyes flashing.

"Off topic? What points did she miss?" I asked softly. I wanted her to play her cards first before I crushed them down like a bulldozer. She took the bait indeed. From her desk she retrieved a notebook in which she listed the points she was expecting in the paper. I indicated that every one of these points was included in Tiffany's paper.

"It... it's not just having the points" said Mrs. Howard. I could tell she was now beginning to get flustered. "It's how they're presented..."

"Yes?" I asked quietly. I was as cool as a cucumber.

"Presentation, grammar, spelling, sentence structure..."

"So where exactly in these areas did Tiffany fail?"

Mrs. Howard was seething at this point. She looked at her watch as if to tell me that this meeting was taking longer than anticipated. She knew she was cornered and didn't like it one bit. "You're not Tiffany's mother, are you?" She was now questioning my authority.

I smiled. "Does she look that much like me? No... I'm her aunt... her guardian." I was becoming adept at these fake smiles. From nowhere, one of Nanny's pet sayings 'Not all skin teet' is laugh' came to mind.

Eventually Mrs. Howard had to admit that Tiffany's grammar was flawless and she had included all the points that were expected. She lost marks for presentation and irrelevance. She couldn't be more specific about presentation. Untidiness maybe, I prompted. Exactly, she answered, glancing at her watch again.

I crossed my legs to get more comfortable. She might as well get used to the fact that I was here for the long haul. "So do you think this paper is untidy?" I asked pointing to the paper on the desk.

"Her handwriting leaves a lot to be desired," replied Mrs. Howard.

"So how much did you deduct for that?"

Mrs. Howard looked at the paper as if she was seeing it for the first time. "Well she got 51%... that's not bad."

I uncrossed my legs. "Not bad that she got the lowest mark in the class?" I asked. "That's terrible." I retrieved

Andrew's paper from my briefcase. "This untidy paper laden with spelling mistakes and grammatical errors, which above all contained half of the points you expected earned 55%... a better mark than Tiffany's."

Mrs. Howard turned beet red. With the evidence in front of her, she was totally exposed.

"Whose paper is this? Where did you get this paper?" Her voice was becoming shrill.

I ignored her question. If I didn't have more photocopied proof in my briefcase and if I wasn't already having a bad day and if Tiffany was not the object of this unfair treatment I would not have come down on Mrs. Howard as harshly as I did. I would not have accused her of being unfair and unjust. I would not have told her she was trying to belittle and demean Tiffany. I would not have bolted up from my chair, collecting the papers from the desk as I threatened to take the matter up with the school principal.

It must have been the getting up from the chair. It was the second time that month, that that action turned things completely around for me. First it was at the car dealership. Now it was with Mrs. Howard. Getting up from the chair combined with the threat to take the matter up with the principal literally had Mrs. Howard, who up to that point had been checking her watch constantly, dashing around the desk to implore me to stay.

Before I left, not only was Tiffany's mark increased to 95%, Mrs. Howard admitted the relevance of Tiffany's research and reference to Mary Secole. Without my asking she even included a brief note of apology to Tiffany. I warned her that in the future I would be very wary - keeping a very watchful eye on all aspects of Tiffany's school life.

Tiffany and I were out celebrating her success. First we went to her favorite seafood restaurant then we visited the mall. I left her to roam the mall without a chaperon while I did some much needed shopping. I could not resist a cute denim purse that I knew Tiffany would love. It was overpriced but I wanted to give her a treat.

An hour later we were reunited. Tiffany pulled me into a pet store, confident now that she was riding high on success. I'd promised to buy her a treat she said, and she wanted a pet.

"A pet?" I objected. I didn't tell her I had already bought her a treat. "Wouldn't you prefer a nice blouse or a purse or..."

"No Aunt Boni... I really would like a pet."

"Come on Tiffany... you know in an apartment you can't have any pets."

"We can have fish," she pointed out. "And we already have a fish tank at home."

Tiffany at one time had a tank full of fish but to her dismay one fish seemed to be absent every time she checked the tank. Regina later discovered that a big fish purchased after the tank had been set up, was feeding on the smaller ones.

"Oh look at these!" she exclaimed, as we got closer to the fish area.

"What's that?" I asked. I absolutely hated pet stores. What if some confounded reptile was on the loose!

"Frogs" she replied. "Aren't they cute Aunt Boni? Can I have some of these?"

"Tiffany... what will your Mum say about these?"

"I'll be the one taking care of them Aunt Boni..."
I wanted out of that place sooner rather than later. So I agreed to buy Tiffany two little pink, transparent looking frogs with food and paraphernalia. I guess as frogs go they were cute. Since according to the instructions which came with them, the food needed to be placed in the tank in one week intervals and Tiffany understood clearly they were not coming to my apartment - we were going straight away to the Southpark apartment to set them up in the fish tank, I agreed to purchase them. If Regina didn't like it, she could do whatever she pleased but I was exercising my guardian privileges to the fullest.

12

When we finally arrived at my apartment, Tiffany wanted to call her mother to share her good news. I couldn't believe that the number Regina left with us was not in service.

"I'm sure your Mum will call you soon Tiffany and then you can tell her," I said with a weak attempt at reassurance.

"I'll call Dad then," she said checking his number in her little address book.

I didn't want to see her bubble burst. "Come look at this little gift I bought you" I interrupted, handing her the parcel with the denim purse I had purchased at the mall.

"Oh thank you Aunt Boni... it's lovely!" she exclaimed, as she quickly examined the purse then deposited a big smack on my cheek. But right away she was back to the phone. Clearly the frogs made more of a hit than this purse.

"Hello Dad."

She'd actually gotten through to her father. They had quite a lengthy conversation, which rather surprised me. I had the impression that Michael was indifferent towards his daughter. From my bedroom I overheard her telling him all about her project and Mrs. Howard and the treats Aunt Boni got for her at the mall. We seemed to have the same attitude towards frogs. "But they're cute, little frogs Daddy," Tiffany laughed as she tried to convince her father. Finally she handed me the phone.

"Dad wants to speak to you," she said.

I took the phone reluctantly. From Regina I had heard only negative things about this man, whom I understood to be a deadbeat dad and had been a cheating husband. I didn't really care to speak to him.

"Boni" he said. "Thanks so much for all you're doing for Tiffany. I just can't thank you enough."

I was dumbfounded. He sounded so earnest, as if he really cared. "Oh... no problem. I love doing stuff with Tiffany... she's like my..." I was about to say daughter. "We're buddies." I corrected myself.

"I can't thank you enough" he repeated. "Going to visit her teacher and all that..."

"No problem," I said again.

There was silence for a while. I was about to give the receiver back to Tiffany when he said "Boni, I'm going away on assignment next week but I'll be back for Thanksgiving and I would love Tiffany to come to visit me in Montreal... with you." Michael worked with the Canadian Military. He was part of the CF18 squadron sent by Canada, under the authority of the United Nations to condemn Iraq's invasion of Kuwait.

"Yes... but what about Regina?" I asked knowing full well that Regina had forbidden him from visiting Tiffany. I didn't know what her attitude would be towards Tiffany visiting her father, whom she had frequently told me was a deadbeat dad.

"Leave it to me... I'll work that out with Regina" he said and I found myself agreeing to his plan.

Regina called on Wednesday. She seemed rushed and didn't have much time to talk to me, so I didn't fill her in on my visit to Mrs. Howard. She was anxious to talk to Tiffany, who hurried out from the shower wrapped in towels to take the call. She was having a good time in Vegas, even though it was work, she told Tiffany. She hoped Tiffany was behaving herself and not giving Aunt Boni too much trouble. Her return journey had to be switched from Sunday to the following Wednesday. She was coming by the 11:00 p.m. flight so Tiffany might as well stay till Thursday with Aunt Boni if it wasn't a problem. It wasn't but I would have appreciated if she'd spoken to me directly. She hastened off the phone assuring Tiffany that she would call again that weekend. I noticed Tiffany did not bother to tell her mother about her new pets.

"Why don't you call Ayanna?" I suggested to Tiffany. "If it's okay with her mum, I'll take you over to visit her this weekend." I remembered how impressed Madge and Willie were at Tiffany's project. Now that the story had a happy ending, I was sure Tiffany would like to relate it to them.

As soon as Madge heard Tiffany's voice on the phone, she right away invited her to come over that Sunday.

"You can spend the day," she said. "Ayanna will be so glad to have you." Ayanna was at her gymnastics class at the time.

Tiffany beamed with delight. I was so happy for her. She needed the companionship of people her age that were not hell bent on leading her down the garden path. I had suggested earlier that she invite a couple 'nice' friends over. Tiffany scoffed at the idea. It dawned on me that my shabby apartment with its old make-do furniture would do more to embarrass Tiffany with her friends than anything else. Oh well!

Ad and I had lunch together in the cafeteria the next day. Her stepdaughter, Sharon, was visiting for the week and as usual posed quite a challenge to Ad and Herbert. In addition to the usual piercings and tattoos, she now sported a halo of pink hair.

"Say thank God... at least she's in university," I said to Ad, wondering to myself whether children really appreciated the stress they put their parents through. "One day she's going to grow up."

"Me t'ink she want freeload off us forever," remarked Ad, as she tossed aside a dried up sandwich. "Pure cardboard," she commented on the lunch she'd picked up in the cafeteria.

"She's a bright girl," I insisted. "One day she's going to find her niche."

"Me hope you right."

I hoped I was right too. Sharon was dramatic and also manipulative. This new look may have been simply to shake the 'bejeepers' out of Ad and Herbie. How disappointed she would have been if they had simply ignored it. But I guess that's easier said than done. I pointed out to Ad that I had noticed an 'artsy' side to her though. It would be nice if that part of her could be encouraged and channeled productively.

The conversation moved to Tiffany. Tiffany and I were actually having a great time together. On Saturday we were going to pick up my new car.
"You know Boni...you should 'a have yoh own pickney years ago."
I laughed loudly. Wasn't she just complaining to me about her pickney?
"An' what about Todd?" I was expecting that question.
"What about him?" I replied. I hadn't heard from Todd since last week when he'd rudely hung up the phone on me after I'd asked him about teaching.
"Erbie say him want you come visit him in Toronto."
When hell freezes over, I thought. To Ad I replied, "You know that's out of the question now...by the way...you want to come with us on Saturday to pick up the *Firefly*?"

Madge invited me for supper when I dropped off Tiffany on Sunday after we'd gone for a spin in the *Firefly*.
"We'd love to have you," she said and since I had nothing more exciting planned that day but cleaning and laundry, I gladly accepted. Besides it felt good driving my shiny new car. Yesterday, Tiffany, Adlyn and I cruised into up-scale neighbourhoods, admiring the beautiful homes, each boasting that mandatory basketball hoop, unused and lonely.
I couldn't wait to show my car to Regina. I felt a slight tinge of regret just thinking of Reg. Until recently we used to be so close. She hadn't called this weekend as she had promised. I wondered what was going on in

her mind. Tiffany definitely seemed more in tune with her dad, who had been calling every couple of days. He knew all about my *Firefly* and that Tiffany was spending Sunday with a friend called Ayanna Johnson. Each time he called he would ask to speak to me and would thank me over and over for the care and attention I was giving to Tiffany.

    I liked Madge and Willie. Their home exuded a warmth and comfort that was palpable. We sat around their dinette table to a delicious meal of 'pepper pot' made by Willie. Tiffany, unlike many children of her generation, was open to trying new and varied foods. Her palate did not respond only to hamburger and fries. For the week she'd been with me, we'd done a fair amount of walking and since I did not keep any whipped cream or syrup in my pantry she'd had to settle for what was there.

    They were delighted with Tiffany's success with her project and told her so. While the girls were in the garden I filled them in on the true story with Mrs. Howard. Willie was not surprised.

    "Like with every occupation" he said, "there are those who shouldn't be there."

    "But should it be a parent's job to find out who should or shouldn't be there?"

    "No" said Willie. "But when you see a sign, you have to follow up on it."

I thought to myself, Regina had not intended to follow up - she had simply intended to let this incident slide by.

    "And that's why I think you guys did such a masterful job," continued Willie. I said nothing. If he only knew. Through the window I could see Ayanna doing cartwheels on the lawn. She was as agile as a butterfly.

"My dear Boni," Madge said. "Unfortunately we can't rely on the school system to truly educate our black children in terms of affirming and dignifying their heritage and culture."

This was getting too deep for me. "Eh?" I asked looking a bit confused. What was I paying taxes for if I couldn't expect the school system to do their job and properly educate the children?

"What you did by getting Tiffany to include Mary Secole in her Nightingale project was dynamite, " Madge continued.

"It certainly blew up in her face. Look at all the trouble it landed her in," I pointed out.

"But you handled it very well" continued Willie. "Some teachers, regardless of where they're from or what colour they are, can be way off base in their thinking process."

I assumed Willie knew what he was talking about, after all he was a teacher himself.

"And the curriculum can be so biased," Madge was saying.

I must have looked totally confused, because Willie hastened to add, "even if the system may be faulty, it is still possible to get from it what is needed and jettison the rest."

"That's right," said Madge. "God knows in our high schools we were fed a lot of irrelevant crap too."

Willie began humming a tune and the words sprung at me right away. I had learned this song as a youngster in school. "Men of Harleck bravely marching..." Madge and I sang along with Willie. Did we know who or what were these men? The point was well made.

I looked out the window at the girls playing outside. Tiffany was trying to catch the falling leaves from the trees. Ayanna was lucky to have two parents that were so vigilant and on top of things. Poor Tiffany! I secretly made a vow to be there for her as much as I could.

Madge was saying something about her friend Jessica. They grew up together in Grenada and went to the same high school. When Jessica and Curt moved to Toronto, where Curt was a criminal lawyer, Madge was deeply disappointed.

"Have you noticed how very well worn that road between Ottawa and Toronto is?" laughed Willie.

"Not only because of Jessica but I also have my sister, Flo, and brother-in-law there," continued Madge. "They have a son Ayanna's age and three younger daughters."

"They must be very busy," I said. I had an image of the lady who lived in a shoe, with so many children she didn't know what to do. To me, in this environment, a family of four children seemed huge. But the closeness between these families was evident. There was a distinct community spirit, despite them living miles apart. Once again I felt a tinge of regret regarding my deteriorating friendship with Regina.

"Do you go to Toronto often?" Madge asked me.

"No," I replied and told them briefly of my last trip there, stressing more the baseball game than anything else. Somehow Todd's name came up. Willie used to know him very well during those years he lived in Ottawa.

"Too bad about that scandal he got involved with," said Madge with a little sigh.

"What scandal?" I asked, a big question mark crumpling my brow as my widened eyes scanned their faces.

Just then both girls burst into the kitchen. Madge looked relieved. She had accidentally put her foot in her mouth.

"Mum, can we have some of your apple pie please?" asked Ayanna.

"Sure sweetie" answered Madge glad for an excuse to spring up from the table.

By the time dessert and coffee were served to everyone, it was time for Tiffany and me to say the good-byes and return home. There was no further mention of Todd or scandals.

13

Regina was furious at me. I was getting deeper and deeper into a pit where she was concerned. She had arrived at her apartment on Thursday morning about two a.m. only to find a big frog flapping around on her brand new sofa. It was almost dead. The fact that the fish tank that had been in her walk-in closet had been taken out and set up on the windowsill with water and twigs and stuff gave her a clue that this was a deliberate act.

Poor Tiffany was at the receiving end of her mother's anger when she arrived home from school that afternoon. Before she could acquaint herself with the expensive, new furniture that was all over the living-dining room area, she was sternly greeted by "What on earth is this?" from her mother, who pointed to the weakly hopping frog she had trapped under a mesh cover.

Tiffany was shocked. Her cute little frogs had more than tripled in size and had hopped out of the tank.

"That's my pet frog," said Tiffany.

"Pet frog? Did you and Aunt Boni do this?"

"Yes" said Tiffany.

"Get it out of here... right now... and clean up the mess on my new couch." Regina was livid.

Tiffany searched in vain for the other frog, without daring to tell her mother that there were two of them. She had no choice but to put the ailing frog out of its misery by flushing it down the john.

Almost in tears, Tiffany called me later. I had truly forgotten about the frogs. I could just imagine Regina's attitude to them. With difficulty I refrained from laughing because Tiffany was so upset, especially as the second frog was still nowhere to be found and Regina didn't even know of its existence.

Mother and Brenda had quite the surprise for me. They said that MLP was getting married in December, just before Christmas.

"To whom?" I asked amazed. I didn't think any two of her children had the same father.

"He's been around for a little while," answered Brenda. "Actually he is the father of her last child." I gathered that Mr. Sylvester was a carpenter who had come from St. Vincent "and fell in love with Patty."

"Anyhow... she want a big wedding and she especially want you there."

"Eh...heh?" I was skeptical. I hoped this guy was sincere and wasn't trying to use Patty. Was he into drugs? Did he want a kidney? Crazy thoughts like children being kidnapped for their organs crept into my head. Was MLP's brood the attraction? What exactly was this fellow up to? Anyhow I suspected Aunt Sybil would keep a vigilant eye out and be on top of things.

"She say Lucille and Stonehead comin' for de weddin'," said Mother.

Lucille and Stonehead were my favorite cousins, but over the years we had grown apart. We hadn't seen each other in more than fifteen years. Correspondence, which at first had been weekly, gradually slipped to the occasional Christmas card and now there was complete silence. It would certainly be nice to get together again with them and reminisce about the good old days but I was in over my head lately. What with my new car and townhouse, I couldn't manage it. I was taking possession of my new home next March - weeks before Mother and Brenda arrived and although I didn't intend to go overboard, it had to be moderately furnished.

"T'ink about it" said Mother. "Life so short..."

Her voice trailed off. I deliberately did not mention anything about the car or house this time, as I got the distinct impression Mother thought I was too consumed with these activities. When I'd called her all excited - full of pride, anxiety and some fear - after the builders had begun work on the townhouses, Mother listened, made a few comments, then simply said to me "All dese t'ings nice Bunny but don't forget... Love is de most important t'ing in life." I determined to keep my mouth shut after that.

Tiffany had forgotten her library book on my coffee table, so since I was passing the Southpark apartment building on my way to work I thought I'd drop it off for her without calling ahead first. Regina answered the buzzer and let me into the building.

"Hi Reg... how are you?" I asked smiling when she let me into her apartment. "Spiffy!" I exclaimed as I looked around her beautifully and expensively refurnished living-dining room area. Even the pictures on the walls were changed. Regina had gone all out. "Very nice," I observed. I decided to forget about our differences - let bygones be bygones. Since Regina had returned from Vegas I hadn't seen or spoken to her until now.

"Sorry Boni... but I'm just about to leave for work. This is an odd time for a visit..." Regina was like a block of ice.

"I'm on my way to work too Reg... but I wanted to drop off Tiffany's library book that she'd forgotten at my place." I pushed the book at her. "Remember, she stayed with me last week?" I added sarcastically as I headed towards the door.

"And how much do I owe you for that?" asked Regina as she picked up her purse from the table and began fumbling in it. Never in the six years I had been baby sitting Tiffany had I taken a red cent from Regina and I felt quite insulted now.

I turned and glared at her. I was tempted to shout the b word at her. Instead I said softly "No thanks," and slammed the door behind me.

I was seething with anger as I left Regina's apartment. But more than anger I felt hurt. After all I'd done for that girl over the years, how could she treat me like an old doormat now? I was glad Mason was not in the unit when I arrived at work. He was a master at picking up on my every mood. No matter how hard I tried, he would have known that I was pissed off about something - badly.

I heard Francine, the nurse in the next unit, complaining loudly about somebody else's incompetence. Lord knows I couldn't take Francine's whining today, so feigning to be busy I thumbed through the daytime planner to see what my schedule was like that day. I noted that Mrs. Dacota, the woman I knew from the "ditch" incident, but who didn't know I knew her, was having her hysterectomy on that day. I hoped things would go much better for her than they were for me.

That afternoon when I arrived home, Tiffany called to thank me for dropping off the library book.
"Your Mum was in a foul mood," I blurted out.
"She's still mad about the frogs," said Tiffany. "Do you know the second one was squished underneath the box with the new vacuum cleaner?"
"Oh?"
"Mum had ordered a new vacuum cleaner and when the janitor delivered it last week, he set it down right on the poor frog."
"Oh?" I said again, visualizing the flattened frog. I didn't know what else to say. But I now had information about the parcel that Todd wanted me to talk to Regina about. Miss Money Bags had bought herself a new vacuum cleaner as well.
"I know that was an accident... but the poor, poor frog," moaned Tiffany.
"I'm sure your Mum will get you some new pets, Tiffany."
"No Aunt Boni... I'm never getting any more pets ... *never* again."
Good idea, I thought to myself, as Tiffany excused herself to take another call that was coming in.

Michael said he was just talking to Tiffany and heard all about the fate of the frogs. He had spoken to Regina earlier about Tiffany coming to visit him in Montreal for Thanksgiving. "She said sure... so long as I didn't expect her to drive Tiffany all the way to Montreal and so long as I didn't expect Tiffany to travel by herself, and so long as Tiffany was back in time for school."

Regina was shocked to discover that Michael had all his ducks in a row. When he told her that I had agreed to drive Tiffany to and from Montreal, she was stunned. No wonder she was so mad at me, when I showed up with Tiffany's library book shortly after that conversation.

So it was arranged that Tiffany and I would drive down to Montreal after work on the Friday afternoon of the Thanksgiving weekend. At work that week I told Adlyn about my plans.

"Good for Tiffany," she said. "So nice dat her father seem to be taking an interest these days."

"Don't forget he's been stationed in the Gulf..." I found myself defending Michael.

Ad herself was traveling to New York with Herbie on that weekend stating that they wanted to do some shopping.

"Shopping with Herbie?" I asked. "That'll be a first." It was a well known fact that to Herbie a trip to the dentist to pull teeth was preferable any day to a shopping expedition.

Ad giggled mysteriously. I knew then that there was more in the mortar than just the pestle.

Todd called. It was several weeks since his last call so I was quite surprised. He made no mention whatsoever of our last conversation. There were no apologies. He talked as though that incident never happened; that he'd never rudely slammed the phone down on me. "The bastard," I thought. He asked again when I was coming back to Toronto. He wanted me to attend some gala event with him. "He's got some nerve," I said to myself but I told him I'd think about it. I wondered again about the scandal Madge had referred to, that he'd been involved in. After a few minutes with him doing most of the talking and guffawing, like Uncle Nat's donkeys braying, I'd had enough.

"Todd, excuse me one second" I said. "Another call is coming in," I lied. I returned a minute later to tell him I needed to take a long distance call that was coming in.

"I'll see you on the weekend BeeBee... I'll be coming to Ottawa," he said just as I was about to hang up.

"Bye Todd" I replied, feeling grateful that on the weekend I'd be high and dry in Montreal.

14

Regina was traveling again. This time she admitted that since Tiffany won't be home, she was going to the Laurentians with a friend. "No point in me hanging around here all by myself," she said to Tiffany.

I picked up Tiffany at their apartment building before going to the gas station to fill up my fiery red *Firefly*. As my coworkers, Mason and Francine teasingly pointed out when they saw the car, I had taken a huge step out of the proverbial box. "One small step for man," laughed Mason "but one giant step for Boni."

I was quite excited as we cruised along the highway, but not more so than Tiffany, whom I noticed was bedecked in her favorite designer V tee shirt. She made me peek at some chocolate chip cookies she'd baked for her dad.

Although it was cold and rainy earlier in the week, the weather forecast for the weekend was promising. As we traveled east along the trans-Canada highway, we admired the red, yellow, orange and green colours of the trees.

"Look at that bright red tree," Tiffany exclaimed. She had forgotten all about the unhappy incident with her pets and was talking a mile a minute about everything else. "Ayanna and her family going to Toronto this weekend" she informed me. "They invited me to come with them, but I couldn't because I was going to visit my dad." I detected a tinge of pride in her voice.

"Next time..."

"That's what Aunt Madge said too."

It was good to see Tiffany happy and self confident. I believe that like plants children need constant nourishment to grow and flourish.

"Dad said he's going to take us to an amusement center."

I wasn't sure about that. I intended to let father and daughter spend as much time together as possible while I checked out furniture stores on the east end of the city. There was one in particular I was keen on. I also brought along a book and some magazines to keep me company.

About six thirty we pulled into the visitor parking lot of Michael's east end apartment complex. He answered the buzzer immediately and said he was coming down to the lobby to meet us. The buildings were only three stories high and seemed new. Michael lived on the top level.

I was checking out the art in the lobby when Tiffany exclaimed and rushed forward into the outstretched arms of her dad.

"Daddy! Daddy!" she shouted.

"So good to see you Tiff," he responded as he hugged her warmly. "My... did you lose weight? You look great." He held her away from him as he admired her, confirming my notion that she had indeed lost a bit of weight recently. Tiffany beamed. "And my dear Boni," he said as he solemnly took my hand and brought it to his lips. "I am in your debt." Although we'd had many phone conversations, it was the first time we were actually meeting face to face. I'm afraid I must have been gaping like a 'bazodee'. The guy was razor sharp. Denzel Washington move over, I said to myself.

Michael insisted on carrying our bags up the stairs to his apartment. Watch your step, he warned adding that the elevator was out-of-order. As he opened his apartment door we were warmly greeted by a delicious smell from the kitchen, situated immediately off to the right. The living-dining area, sparsely but adequately furnished, was straight ahead. Michael led us to the left, past the bathroom and deposited Tiffany's bag in one of two bedrooms. In the second bedroom, which he obviously used as an office, and in which there was a pullout couch, he placed my bag.

"I don't mind doubling up with Tiffany," I told him not wanting to deprive him of both bedrooms. The hard looking couch in the living room didn't seem cushy enough to spend a night.

"You guys are my honoured guests this weekend," he replied, "and I want you to be as comfortable as possible." There was a formality about him that really impressed me. Maybe that was something he picked up from the army.

"Look what I brought you, Dad," said Tiffany as she produced the container with the chocolate chip cookies she'd made.

"What a girl... who made these?"

"I made them myself... you can have one now," said Tiffany excitedly.

"We'll have them for dessert," said Michael as he took the container and gave Tiffany a 'thank you' hug. "Give me five minutes to get supper on the table."

"Let me help," I offered and ignoring his protests followed him to the kitchen.

Supper, which consisted of curry goat with rice and peas, fried plantains and cabbage salad had been ordered from a nearby take-out West Indian restaurant. Tiffany and I were both very hungry and settled down to do ample justice to it.

During the meal Tiffany and Michael talked non-stop about school, books and her new friend Ayanna. There was a carefree and jovial banter between them that was heart-warming to see. Tiffany became serious for a moment as she asked her father whether he was scheduled to be posted abroad again. Michael explained that he didn't know. His unit represented Canada in peacekeeping initiatives under the direction of the UN and NATO. Their purpose in the Gulf last August was to aid the gathering coalition forces.

"When duty calls, we must answer," he concluded as he skillfully turned the spotlight on to me. "So Boni, how's everything at your work?"

"Fine," I said. "Just very busy these days."

"Dad... you know Aunt Boni is building a new house?"

He didn't. "That's a great achievement," he said earnestly. "Especially for someone as young as you."

He obviously didn't know how *young* I was and I wasn't going to tell him.

"Well... it's being built. I'm not actually building it."

Michael smiled at me sending a flutter up my spine. I had to remind myself that this guy was a no-good SOB, as Regina had so often told me.

"And her mother and sister are coming to visit next year," continued Tiffany.

"Yes?... I hope I get the opportunity to meet them," said Michael earnestly.

How on earth did he expect to do that, I wondered.

We chatted until almost midnight. Michael was born in Montreal. After many years in Montreal, his father and mother, from Barbados and Trinidad respectively, returned to live in Barbados. Even though his father passed away a few years ago, his mother still continued to live in Barbados. She never returned to Trinidad because of issues regarding a younger sister, ostracized from the family when she had a child out of wedlock. His mother regretted even up to this day that she never got to speak to her sister who died shortly after the baby's birth. Michael showed me pictures of his parents and of his mother with her younger sister when they were teenagers. They both, especially the younger sister, looked so familiar, I felt I already knew them.

It was way beyond Tiffany's bedtime, but who was checking.

"Pass me another of those delicious cookies," Michael said to me, as Tiffany gushed with delight.

I was feeling so comfortable with Michael that I divulged my plan to check out furniture stores the next day. I needed just about everything for my new home, I told him.

"Let's go to *De Leon's*," said Michael taking me by surprise. I was planning on checking out the stores by myself. "It's an excellent place. That's where I bought your bedroom set Tiff."

Tiffany's eyes widened. "Mum said she got it in Montreal."

Michael frowned. "That's right. It did come from Montreal," he said as he slowly shook his head. I saw it clearly now. Regina had taken all the credit for Tiffany's bedroom set and everything else and I had believed her. She had deliberately misled her friends into believing Michael was a deadbeat dad.

Tiffany slept for the entire journey back to Ottawa. We'd had a fantastic weekend with her father, who turned out to be a kind and compassionate man. On Saturday we'd checked out furniture stores and went shopping for books, CDs, as well as children's clothes. This guy was no Herbie. He knew style as well as quality. Later that evening, we visited an amusement center. I couldn't believe how much fun Tiffany had going on all those painful looking rides with her father, who was just as crazy about them as she was. From the safety of a nearby bench I opted to look on. Tiffany went to bed even later than the previous night. She was totally and happily exhausted.

Michael got up early on Sunday morning to put the turkey into the oven. We had a sumptuous turkey dinner that day and later attended a gospel concert at a community church. Like everyone else in the audience, we were at the edge of our seats enjoying the soulful sounds emanating from the choir.

"I love it!" Tiffany exclaimed more than once to Michael.

We said hello to Veronique, whom I was meeting for the first time and who had also attended the concert and was overjoyed to see Tiffany.

"Is years since I lay me eyes on dis chile," she said and stunned me when she added "I hear you taking very good care of her." She was a serious faced woman with worry lines permanently etched on her forehead. She seemed to have much more information on me than I did on her. She inquired about Adlyn and Herbert.

I was glad Tiffany was asleep now as I drove back to Ottawa, so I could be alone with my own thoughts. This past weekend certainly changed the course of my life.

It started on Sunday night. I must have been having a nightmare, when I was awakened by Michael shaking me gently.

"Boni... Boni... wake up," he said.

"What's the matter?" I asked still dazed as I sat up in bed.

"You were screaming," he answered. "I think you were dreaming."

"Oh my God... I'm so sorry." I was overcome with embarrassment.

"Don't worry... I do that sometimes too," said Michael softly as he sat on the bed and placed his arms around me. I snuggled in like a caterpillar in a cocoon.

"Did I disturb Tiffany too?"

I don't remember what he'd answered, but I was aware that his arms around me had felt good. Then suddenly his lips on my face, neck, and to my lips had felt even better as Michael had settled in beside me.

I glanced at my smiling face in the rear view mirror now. Was I the same person who'd told Adlyn that I believed in going very slowly with relationships? Well I guess I lied. Big time!

The rest of that day had been marvelous. The sun had come out with extra brilliance to match the warm glow in my heart.

"Let's go for a walk," Michael had suggested that morning but Tiffany had declined. She'd started on a new book and was quite engrossed in it. So Michael and I went together for a long walk. With Tiffany not there I felt free to ask all about his experiences in Kuwait. Was he ever scared? Did he experience any Gulf War Syndrome? Yes, he did have the occasional nightmare and screaming but since I also experienced these, he wasn't sure it was GWS he said with a smile as he looked at me. My world was turning upside down. This was the same guy that had cheated on Regina with their next door neighbour. Surely he was not to be trusted. What on earth was I doing?

"Boni," he said, as we came through a clearing into a deserted wooded area. "I think you may have heard a lot of negatives about me." He was also a mind reader. "I sure hope you'll give me a chance to prove myself."

"You've already shown me you're a wonderful father," I said seriously.

"I'd like to show you much more than that Boni," he said as he stopped walking and drew me closely to him. The air around us suddenly became overheated. "I've never met a more beautiful, more exquisite woman than you - both inside and out," he continued. Lord, help me! I could listen to this man for all eternity. In the shade beneath the trees our arms encircled each other and our lips met and united as profoundly as did our souls.

"Aunt Boni," Tiffany was now awake. "If Mum isn't at home when we get there, can you come in and stay with me for a while?"

It was close to nine o' clock. We'd encountered a fair amount of traffic on our way back to Ottawa. Regina would most likely be back from the Laurentians now and the last thing I wanted was another show down with her, especially now that I was seriously involved with her ex.

"I have to get ready for work tomorrow," I answered. "But I'll keep you company on the phone, if you wish."

"Okay," said Tiffany, then a minute later added "We can have a three way with Dad. He'll want to know that we arrived safely."

"Okay," I answered.

15

It was getting colder now. I still walked to work everyday, since the only available car parking was in a muddy field at least five minutes from the hospital and since I didn't want to reverse the benefits to my body that had been gained from a twenty-minute walk twice a day. I decided I wouldn't fix what wasn't broke.

With my nurse's uniform, nylons etc... in my backpack, I headed out the door dressed in a warm jogging suit and nylon jacket. It had rained earlier in the morning and there was a fresh smell in the air but the fallen leaves on the sidewalk could be treacherous. I reminded myself to be careful.

After Tiffany hung up the phone and went to bed last night, Michael and I had remained on the line for several hours. We both had important commitments the following day. I could count on the clinic being extra busy after a long weekend. Michael was scheduled to travel to Petawawa early the next morning. We kept telling each other "Darling, I'm going to let you go now," or "It's time for you to get some sleep now, sweetheart" but some force greater than ourselves kept the conversation going on and on. There was so much we wanted to discover and to say to each other.

In the locker room I changed into my uniform then stopped at the coffee shop for a decaf before going up to my unit.

"Another day, another dollar," droned Francine, the nurse in the unit beside me. I smiled at her. Not even Francine's negativity could wipe the smile off my face today.

Mason rushed in shortly after.

"Hi *chèrie*" he said to me as he took out a small comb from his pocket and passed it a few times over his sparse skull. "Did you have a good weekend?"

"Oh yes," I answered. "Did you?" Usually it annoyed me when Mason chose to comb his hair in the unit. I would secretly wonder if he really thought those few long strands of hair he insisted on combing over his bald spot were fooling anyone.

"*Pas mal*," he answered, then looking at my cheerful face observed, "You look... different...very well rested today." Not bad for someone who had been up talking until the wee hours of the morning. But yes, I did feel very well rested indeed.

Todd left a very sullen message on my answering machine. He'd come to Ottawa on Saturday but no one seemed to be around. "You knew I was coming BeeBee ...I told you," he said rather accusingly. He'd called Ad and Herbie and they weren't at home. He'd also called Madge and Willie and they didn't return his calls either. Neither did Regina, who owed him money. "BeeBee, ask her to call me okay?" Was he implying that there was a huge conspiracy against him led by me?

I didn't see Adlyn until later that week. She and Herbie had had a great time in New York, she said. They'd even met up with Sharon there. Interesting, I thought. The shopping went fine, she reported, causing me to take another look at her. Was she serious? Shopping with Herbie went fine? Even for something as personal as a birthday or Christmas present for Ad, Herbie consistently relied on either myself or Regina to help him out. So she couldn't fool me. Whatever they bought in New York was being shipped to them, she said rather mysteriously.

"So how t'ings went in Montreal?"
I knew she was trying to dodge the 'shopping' subject.

"Fine... everything was fine," I answered. I could be mysterious too.

"How Michael?"

"Great... just great...Tiffany had a ball with her dad." I think I was talking much too quickly.

"An' you?" Ad was looking at me curiously. Thank God for dark skin - had I been a white person, it would have been beet red now.

"What about me?" I asked.

"You din have a ball wid 'im too?" She was smiling suspiciously at me.

"Sure... we went shopping and to an amusement center, then to a gospel concert... we all had a great time." I tried to answer nonchalantly.

"Nothin' more dan dat?"

"And we met up with Veronique. She asked about you and Herbie."

"Me talk to Veronique last week. Nothin' more?"

"Absolutely nothing."

"Okay, if you say so," Ad giggled mischievously.

Tiffany showed up at my apartment on Friday afternoon with a head full of fine, intricate braids. It must have taken someone forever to do it.

"Aunt Ad did it," she told me.

"Aunt Ad? When?"

"She did the front on Wednesday evening," said Tiffany. "And I wore the back in a ponytail, and yesterday she finished the back."

So Ad had been in touch with Tiffany, who no doubt told her all about our Montreal trip.

"Did you tell her all about your weekend in Montreal?"

"Mmhmm."

"The amusement center and the gospel concert?" I prompted.

"Oh yes... and the shopping... I told Aunt Ad how I got a new *Betty Hasting* book which I finished on Sunday morning while you and Dad were out walking." So that was it. Ad had put two and two together and was trying to see how much I was prepared to let her in on.

"How's school?" I asked changing the conversation.

"Great," answered Tiffany. "You know Aunt Boni... they've chosen for the Christmas concert, and I have a part."

"Yes?" I was happy for Tiffany.

"I'll be singing a solo," explained Tiffany.

"That's great Tiff!" I exclaimed as I hugged her. "Don't forget to let your dad know. Maybe he can come. I'm sure he'd love to hear you sing." I was certain that

Michael would be very impressed and if at all possible would like to attend - especially if Regina was not going to be there.

During one of our nightly conversations he told me that he and Regina had had a stormy relationship, at best. "We both made a lot of mistakes," he said. "I'm not excusing my own behavior, which was terrible." That I knew. When he'd first met Regina, he was attracted by her pretty face and shapely body. "I've now learned that what you see is just the tip of the iceberg... what's beneath the surface is far more important." When Tiffany came along, soon after they'd been married, he was enthusiastic about being a father. He loved her dearly. He didn't understand though why a baby had to have a million expensive outfits, all bought from that exclusive store *Mother Goose*. That didn't make sense to me either, especially as in three months the baby would have most certainly outgrown those outfits. Regina accused him of being cheap. That was so familiar. Pretty soon they were fighting about money all the time. Then he discovered she'd 'maxed out' all their credit cards. They were close to financial ruin. It took its toll on the relationship but he hung in there.

He was devastated when she left with Tiffany. By then they were hardly on speaking terms. However, he was determined to remain a part of his daughter's life, which Regina made increasingly more difficult for him, even though he paid child support every month. Child support? I had been misled to believe that Michael contributed not a single dime to his daughter's upkeep.

I was not invited to the dinner party Regina had last Saturday evening at her apartment. I heard it was a small party but nevertheless I was not among the invited. I suspected Adlyn and Herbie were included only because Herbie did the catering. Very present was McIvor Drayer, Regina's new beau, a few of his cronies as well as people she'd met through her workplace. She was moving in totally different circles now.

Regina had once told me that unless she was very serious she would never bring anyone she was dating to her home or allow that person to meet Tiffany. "I don't want to confuse my child," she'd told me. So I guessed she was serious about this new guy.

"Regina get herself ah sugar daddy," Ad said to me last week. Although curious, I didn't want to ask any questions. I let Ad do the talking. "Is ah ol' baldie she goin' wid. Me t'ink he workin' for de Government."

As usual Michael and I spent that Saturday night talking to each other on the phone.

"You know what's going on with Regina?" he asked me. "She's been hounding me down for money recently."

"Whaaat?" I thought she had a sugar daddy.

"She claims what I'm sending for Tiffany is just not enough. Tiffany's needs are a lot more now. She has grown out of all her winter clothes and…"

I began to laugh. "She certainly has enough to throw a dinner party tonight," I observed.

It was Michael's turn to stutter. "Whaaat?"

"You heard me."

"And don't tell me you declined her invitation."

"What invitation?" I replied. "I'm afraid I didn't make her guest list."

Michael remained silent for a while. I could tell he was taking this in, trying to process it. Finally he spoke.

"Boni..." he began slowly. "I don't care about any silly dinner party but I know that for years you have been Regina's right hand... helping her with Tiffany." He stopped. I could visualize him shaking his head. "What's going on honey?"

I really didn't know and at that particular time I didn't give two hoots.

16

After only two weeks in Petawawa, Michael called to say he was being sent to Croatia as part of the Canadian peacekeeping mission there. It amazed me how distraught I felt. I took slight comfort in the fact that he was taking two days off and was coming to visit Tiffany and me. He hoped he would be back from Croatia before Christmas. He was even hoping to attend Tiffany's Christmas concert.

I hadn't told anyone about our involvement. Even though we spoke on the phone every night, it was a precious secret that I cherished deeply and for the time being wanted to keep in the secret folds of my heart.

The very next day I got some more bad news. In a phone call from Brenda I learned that Uncle Nat had passed away. The funeral was scheduled for that Saturday. Uncle Nat had been my favorite uncle - in many ways I was closer to him than to my own father and was deeply saddened by this news. I called to express my condolences to Aunt Sybil and to my

Beneath the Surface

surprise, Uncle Benny's wife, Aunt Theresa, answered the phone.

"We ol' heads movin' on," she said to me sadly. I had never before known Aunt Theresa to visit either Nanny or Uncle Nat in Côte St. Pierre. As Nanny once put it, "Theresa and Sybil cyan' agree on nuttin'. If one o' dem say peas, de odder boun' to say corn." The fact that Aunt Theresa was there now, in their hour of grief, was significant. She told me that everyone, especially Uncle Benny and my mother, was taking Uncle Nat's passing very badly.

I dreaded calling Mother. She was sure to imply that I should put everything down and fly home for my uncle's burial. Without her saying it, I would feel that I was too mercenary, not putting sufficient emphasis on the important things in life. Of course I went home for my father's funeral but Nanny had quietly slipped away in her sleep the day after I left Grenada and I was in the middle of final exams when I received the news of Sister Baby's passing. I was sure that if I called Mother now to try and cheer her up I would surely be more disheartened before the conversation was finished.

But I would have dearly loved to be with Lucille and Stonehead to mourn the passing of Uncle Nat. I hadn't seen them in more than fifteen years and most certainly they would be traveling from California and London to their father's funeral. Not to mention Patty and her numerous children - all of dubious fatherhood. Poor Patty! She wasn't playing with all her marbles. I remember her complaining to me that her parents bossed her around too much, a lot more so than they did Lucille, her younger sister. Even Lucille tried to boss her around too, she said indignantly, pushing out her bottom lip. "But watch me now nuh." I waited. "I ha' somebody to call me Mudder," she added proudly with her arms akimbo. "I ha' three babies an' Lucille don' even ha' boo." She looked at me expecting a show of reverence for her lofty accomplishment in life. One more nut and Patty would have been a fruit cake. I returned a blank stare. At that time there were Mavis, Gladys and Willis. Since then she'd added Alice, Francis, Janice, Davis and Beatrice earning for herself the nickname MLP - Minister of Labour and Production - from some folks. Well, Patty had recently announced her upcoming marriage to a fellow from St. Vincent. Too bad, Uncle Nat was not going to be around for her wedding.

Uncle Nat's two oldest sons, Gabe and Donald left home as young men to work in the Virgin islands. Letters which initially were scarce, ceased altogether after a few years. No one knew their whereabouts although from time to time there would be rumours of sightings in the Bahamas or New York, even Vancouver. Despite his handicap, Clyde was proving more and more to be the one who most closely followed in his father's footsteps. He was both practical and hard-working.

I looked out the window of my Ottawa apartment at a gray November day. I sighed loudly and without my being fully conscious of it the tears ran steadily down my cheeks.

"Tell me about your uncle," Tiffany said when she visited me later that day and found me in a sad and morose mood. Bless her heart, she was doing her best to lift my spirits.

"Uncle Nat was a kindhearted, little man. He was just about so high..." I gesticulated with my hand. "But strong and wiry. He was the life of the village. Whenever anyone needed something done, Uncle Nat was the man. He was doctor, butcher, farmer, carpenter, you name it..." I smiled inwardly as I recalled my uncle. He was not a formally educated man - he may not have known the correct use of the subjunctive in a sentence nor pondered the benefits of space programs which test frog reproduction at zero gravity, but practical and intelligent he certainly was. He was a solid man. "He was the architect and builder of his own brick home. I remember him helping with the butchering of pigs and cows... I can picture him cutting cane in the fields or laying out nutmeg and cocoa in the boucan to dry."

"What's a boucan?" asked Tiffany.
How could I explain this simply? "A boucan is a huge drying tray placed on rails, so that it can easily be pushed under a building in case of rain or be locked up at night for security."

"So it was used to dry cocoa and nutmeg?"
"Primarily. It could also be used to dry sapote and tonka beans."

"How did Uncle Nat act like a doctor?"
"Well maybe I should say semi-doctor," I replied. "He bandaged all bruises and cuts, removed jiggers..."

"What are jiggers?" asked Tiffany.
It dawned on me that I hardly knew what jiggers were myself. "It's a minute insect that can burrow into your foot, especially between toes, causing an itching like you won't believe. You get it by walking barefoot in unsanitary sandy places." I didn't know whether this

was correct but it sounded feasible. I continued my description of Uncle Nat.

"He also administered different herbal remedies for various aches and maladies but most of all after holidays, just before school reopened, he would give all the children a dose of worm medicine." I frowned as I remembered this routine. I didn't know which was worse; the smell or the taste of that thick gooey medicine. The adults claimed this was to ensure we children were purged of any worms that may have entered our bodies from all the rotten fruit we may have carelessly ingested during our holidays. Indeed, it would have been a challenge to any worm to hang in there while one's intestines exploded in the latrine several times that day. But I was convinced that having worms was a better deal to taking that nasty medicine. Consequently I always tried to head back home to St. George's just before worm medicine time.

"Were you ever around when Uncle Nat butchered an animal?"

"Of course... many times," I responded cheerily. I told Tiffany all about the smoking of hams and how some of the tripe and the bony parts were salted and placed in a thick earthenware jar for later consumption.

"What did they do with the rest of the tripe?" Tiffany wanted to know. She didn't say so but I knew while she was intrigued by it, all this 'tripe' talk was somewhat disgusting to her.

"That's what we made blood pudding with," I told her.

"Aunt Boni did they throw out any part of the pig at all?"

Just the look on Tiffany's face as she wrinkled her brows and opened her eyes widely had me doubled over shaking with laughter. Eventually we were both laughing so hard, I almost missed hearing the door buzzer. Adlyn had come over with quite the surprise for me.

"Y'all havin' a joke fest or somet'ing?" said Ad, noticing that we had both been laughing heartily.

"Actually I just got some sad news," I said as I wiped my eyes. I told her about Uncle Nat's death.

"Me so sorry to hear dat."

"But Tiffany couldn't have done a better job of cheering me up." I reached over and hugged Tiffany.

"What's this?" I asked as Ad took from her purse and handed me a square envelope elegantly tied with beautiful purple and yellow ribbon. If Ad and Herbie weren't already married I would have guessed this was a wedding invitation. Sharon maybe?

"You de first one to get dis," said Ad smiling mysteriously as she waited for my reaction.

I started to slowly untie the ribbon.

"Save the ribbon Aunt Boni... I could use it in my hair."

Ad laughed. Finally I had the envelope opened and took out a beautiful yellow card, which in purple lettering cordially invited me to attend the pre-opening of a new restaurant *The Caribbean Kitchen* on 123 Eastern Road in Ottawa on December 1st. I was flabbergasted.

"Whaat?" I stammered as I hugged Ad and danced her around my tiny living room.

"You have a restaurant, Aunt Ad?"

"Not me darlin'... Uncle Erbie."

I was so happy for them. "Did that trip to New York have anything to do with this?"

"Of course," said Ad. "More dan one time me almos' spill all de beans to you."

"That so?"

"We had to go shop... and you not gwine believe jus' how helpful Sharon was wid all dat stuff. You know ... is she do dese invitations."

I was impressed but again I always felt beneath that rough façade that Sharon liked to project, there was something absolutely splendid.

I was giving my apartment a much needed cleaning. Michael was visiting for the first time and I didn't want him to think less of me. The guy had me firmly placed on a pedestal and I wanted to stay right there as long as possible. When he heard of my uncle's death, he arranged to come over a day earlier to be with me. So he was coming over tomorrow morning and I was trying to get a few things ready. I had already informed Mason that I needed a vacation day.

"A vacation day?"

"Yes," I replied a little irritably. I had been doing more than my fair share of filling in for sick time taken by Francine and other staff recently. "It may well have been a week to go to my uncle's funeral... but I think just a day will do me." I nipped any further questions or objections in the bud.

I was about to slip out to the liquor store to get some wine and pick up a few items at the grocery store, when the phone rang.

"BeeBee, sorry to hear of your uncle's death," said Todd.

"Thanks Todd." I guessed he'd been speaking to Herbie or Adlyn.

"I would like to come and cheer you up..."

"Todd please... I'm fine."

"You know BeeBee... I know I was... I could be a little grumpy sometimes..."

Was this a belated kind of apology? "Eh heh?"

"I would like to make it up to you BeeBee."

"Todd... trust me... I'm fine. You don't have to make anything up to me."

He remained silent for a moment. I was just about to excuse myself when he said "Adlyn told me all about the restaurant...isn't that something?"

"Yes... it's great. I'm truly happy for them."

"You know how long I been telling Herbie to do that?"

"Eh heh?"

"Years now I been telling Herbie that's what he should do."

"Well he's doing it now."

"But look how much time de man waste nuh."

"Better late than never," I applied the old cliché.

"She said my invitation for the pre-opening party in the mail."

"That's good."

"So I'll be seeing you then BeeBee. Can hardly wait. Sounds like it's going to be one bash of a fête."

"Got to run now Todd," I said as I hung up the receiver. Damn it! Damn it! Damn it!

17

For most people in Northern climates February is the most depressing month of the year. For me the most dismal month is November - when the temperature begins to hover around zero with increased frequency and when nights have become longer than days; it's dark when leaving for work in the morning and it's dark when returning home after work.

Both high and low points graced this past November. Those two glorious days Michael and I spent together in my little apartment before he took off to Croatia embodied them both. The flame within me had erupted into a full blown fire. Together in our hearts a little orchestra was created; each heart string separate yet relating to all others in triumphant symphony.

Michael took Tiffany for breakfast the morning before he left, and promised her he would be back soon - hopefully by Christmas. Despite the tugging of our hearts neither of us dared be so hopeful.

Secretly, I was a basket case by the time Michael was ready to leave. It helped to remind myself that he was experienced at this, he'd been present in the Gulf war, where Canadian forces had suffered no casualties and quite frankly he was doing what he wanted to do. I took some comfort in the fact that the Canadian military was predominantly peacekeepers in the world and not aggressive testosterone-fueled warmongers. But it was impossible to shake that nagging feeling of depression that was threatening to engulf me. I felt it more acutely than ever one particular evening when I arrived home from work.

    I decided to go jogging. Physical exercise has a way of realigning the disconnected spirit. So I put on my jogging attire, slipped on a headband to protect my ears, got out my running shoes and headed out the door.

    I started down Hilton street. Fifteen minutes later I was passing the Southpark apartment buildings where Regina and Tiffany lived. I turned on to an area with town houses, the lights from which reflected onto the streets. Some cooking smells escaped through tightly closed doors or windows to my nostrils causing feelings of hunger to overcome me. To fight these hunger pangs I decided to cut across through an alley to Ainsley park by the river. The air was fresh there. I was well warmed up now and I'd gotten my stride on. I breathed deeply in and out, allowing fresh air to fill up and be expelled from my lungs. Already I could feel my body relax wonderfully. I loved the natural feeling of this park. It was so beautiful.

    I was just about to cross over from the river path back on to Ainsley road, when as I turned the corner I quite suddenly almost collided with someone. The person held on to me briefly, perhaps to steady himself. "So sorry," I apologized as what I assumed was a gold tooth glittered briefly in the sparse light. He didn't apologize. I kept going not wanting to stop my stride but I did look back briefly. A tall, gaunt individual dressed in loose fitting dark clothes, with long blondish hair falling from a black tuque, was staring in my direction. "Gawd," I said to myself. "If this guy was in Côte St. Pierre, he would certainly be *La Diablesse* material." I didn't know then how important my looking back, ever so briefly, would prove to be.

The Caribbean Kitchen although small was artistically and beautifully decorated. My jaw literally fell open when I learned that Herbie's daughter, Sharon, was responsible for the theme and decor. Caribbean paintings and artifacts decorated the walls and from the low ceiling hung fish nets with various conch and other sea shells. Hibiscus flowers formed the centerpieces on the tables.

Decked off in a beautiful low cut red gown, Ad made a splash as the hostess of the restaurant's pre-opening party. She was a full-figured woman that truly appreciated her body. She greeted everyone with warmth and exuberance as they entered.

While waiting to be seated, guests were treated to hors d'oeuvres while they mingled with one another and Caribbean music played softly in the background. There were about fifty guests present altogether.

I sat on a long table with Madge and Willie Johnson, Madge's sister Fleurina with her husband Chester, as well as Jessica and Curt Lincoln. There was something so chic and refined about the Toronto folks. We were later joined by Veronique from Montreal, who wanted to know how Tiffany and Michael were doing. I regretted Michael couldn't be with me but trusted we would have many occasions like this in the future.

It was great seeing Jessica and Curt again. On Jessica's right arm chimed the usual array of bracelets. They introduced me to their children Joshua and Jolene, seated at a nearby table with Sharon and some other young people. Josh and Jo were the epitome of beauty and dignity. I knew they were both successful in school and frankly, I thought to myself, if Curt and Jessica had placed a specific order with God, they could not have been more fortuitous.

Fleurina was taller than her sister and more on the slim side but one couldn't miss the familial resemblance. Chester's short, stocky build had me thinking that these two sisters should do some mate swapping. Willie's height would certainly complement Fleurina's stall stature, while Chester and Madge were both inclined to be short and stout.

Fleurina was a warm and happy woman - even more so than her sister. When we were introduced, she shocked me by telling me she remembered when I was born. "It was around *Janet* time," she said. "I remember your grandmother walk all the way to St. George's from Côte St. Pierre. She stopped off for the night up the hill at Ma Hilly, Jessica's grandmother." I was truly amazed at her memory. Fleurina and I also had something else in common - we were both nurses. At least until recently she used to be a nurse at the *People's* hospital in Toronto. After her third child was born, she and Chester decided that she would become a stay-at-home mom.

"I hear you have a son and three daughters," I told her.

"Yes my dear... after years of thinking we weren't going to be parents..."

"You miss work?" asked Veronique who had joined us.

"Not at all," replied Fleurina. "I enjoy being at home for the children... and you know I'm back to dress designing and dressmaking... which I love."

"Did you make this dress?" I asked. Fleurina was wearing an elegant black dress, which fitted at the hips and cascaded around her calves.

"Oh yes," she answered, and surprised me even more when she mentioned she'd also made the two piece silk outfit Jessica was wearing.

"It so good dat you able to be home wid de children," said Veronique, steering the conversation away from dressmaking. She herself was a single parent of two teenagers.

Fleurina nodded. "I believe what children need most of all is time with their parents, and since we can manage it..."

She was a simple, down-to-earth and very gifted woman. I was truly impressed with her and actually with the couple. Before Fleurina left her job at *People's*, Chester had taken some leave of absence from his work to stay home with the children.

Distinguished dignitaries from the city and the Caribbean community also graced this occasion. Herbert was like a brand new person. In formal chef's attire from time to time he proudly came out from the behind-the-scenes area to greet his guests and receive their heartfelt congratulations.

Todd, conspicuously dressed in a winter white suit, arrived late and loud as usual. He came over to our table to say hello to everyone. I was glad there was no more room at our table and he had to sit elsewhere. He seemed quite at home with the folks at his table though. Noticeably absent were Regina and her date, whom I knew Ad had invited.

As expected the meal served by two uniformed waitresses was delicious. If this was a sample of what this restaurant would provide, it was sure to do well. Before dessert was served it was time for the official welcome and thank you from Adlyn and Herbie. On a few occasions I had noticed Herbie retrieve his speech, several pages of it, from the pocket of his jacket for a sneak practice. Sharon received loud cheering and clapping when Adlyn pointed out her responsibility for the restaurant's decor. The representative from the city, the Caribbean dignitaries present, as well as a few guests gave their congratulations, best wishes and promises of support to Ad and Herbert.

By midnight the party was over and just about everyone had said their good byes and left. I saw Todd leave with a young lady from the table where he'd been sitting. Great, I thought. Now he'll leave me alone. Ad had slipped from her high heels into some flats and with myself and Sharon assisted Herbie and the two waitresses with the cleaning up.

Exhausted and happy, we all sat around to do a post mortem.

"That was an excellent party," I said. "And Sharon girl you're bursting with talent."
Sharon smiled cautiously. Tonight her hair was short and reddish black. Her lipstick, eye makeup and nail polish were a stunning black.

"Everyt'ing went off so well," said Ad.
I complimented both Ad and Herbie on their great

speeches. I noticed Ad completely refrained from using her *patoi s*during her speech.

"Let's have one for de road," said Herbie enthusiastically, as he poured from a liqueur bottle into some tiny glasses.

"You not drivin' tonight Erbie?" asked Ad viewing the bottle.

"He sure got to drive me home," said the younger of the two waitresses. "After that mess in the park last night..."

"What mess?" asked Sharon.

"You didn't hear? A girl got stabbed in the park last night."

"Which park?" I asked. "Last night I went jogging in Ainsley park."

The young waitress looked at me with dilated pupils.

"I think that's the park where the stabbing took place," she said softly.

In bed that night my mind replayed the events of the past few days. I hoped *The Caribbean Kitchen* would do well. I knew the quality of the food would be superb. That's the first place I'd be taking Michael to when he returns home. I should be hearing from him tomorrow. I'll tell him all about Herbie's pre-opening party for his restaurant. My prediction about Sharon was coming true in slow motion. Even though she tried not to seem impressed, I knew she glowed inwardly whenever someone complimented her.

I thought of the stabbing in Ainsley park. The only person I saw in the park when I jogged through there the previous night was that tall, *La Diablesse* looking guy. I could picture him clearly in my mind.

Something flashed in his mouth; I assumed it was a gold tooth. He did come into my path rather unexpectedly and I actually remembered him touching me. Was that the park stabber? I wondered suddenly. Could I have been the intended victim but I was too fast for him? I instantly felt cold and scared and overcome by a sick feeling to my stomach.

18

I went over to Madge and Willie's home the next day to visit with the Toronto folks before their return journey later that day. I took Fleurina up on her suggestion that I come over for her to take my measurements, just in case some time in the future I wanted an outfit made. An offer like that I could not refuse. So without hesitation I seized the opportunity. Joshua, with Jolene right behind him, answered the doorbell.

"Hello," "Hi Boni," they both greeted me pleasantly as Jolene took my coat and led me into the living area where the others were huddled in quite a tizzy. Curt was on the phone to someone and it seemed serious.

"Where is he now?" I heard him say. "Okay... I'll be right over."

I greeted everyone just as Curt was hanging up the receiver. He'd been talking with Herbert about Todd apparently.

"I'll come with you," said Chester, who was already in his coat. Curt and Chester headed out the door.

News of the park stabbing was in the local newspapers, a copy of which lay open on the living room table. I felt that queasy sensation return to my stomach. The victim, a young woman who was now in the intensive care unit of the *Universal* hospital, had also been raped. Apparently she had used the words 'black' and 'tall' to the police, who were now searching for someone fitting that description. Herbie had called to say that Todd had been picked up earlier that morning and questioned.

"All he was doing was getting into his car at the corner of Ainsley and Forest," said Madge. A moment later she looked uncomfortably at me as if she'd put her foot in her mouth.
I came to her rescue. "I think that's where the young lady he was cozying up to last night lives," I said. I wanted to disabuse them of any notion that I was involved with Todd. They seemed to get it at last.

"Did they think that whoever did the stabbing would still be in the area waiting to be caught?" asked Jolene sarcastically.

"It didn't help that Todd had been implicated in a rape scandal before," said Fleurina.

"What rape scandal?" I asked her. Everyone but me seemed to know what she was talking about.

"At the school where he'd been working as a substitute teacher, a young girl had accused Todd of rape," Fleurina explained.
This was incredulous. "Yes?" I asked. "Did the case go to court?"

"Yes but it was eventually dropped," answered Jessica. "Todd's story was that the girl was angry because she didn't get the mark she wanted on a certain test."

"She boldly went over to his apartment one evening and demanded that he improve her mark. When he refused she accused him of rape," continued Madge.

"She even had a friend backing up her story," said Fleurina.

"You're kidding."

"The case was ultimately thrown out of court," said Willie. "But it still hurt him."

"In what way?"

"He became an untouchable," said Willie.

"He was already having difficulty getting a contract. After that incident he couldn't even get substitute positions in the city," added Madge.

"Eventually he made the decision to give up teaching altogether."

"He had to dump his career?"

"He was so disillusioned..." answered Madge.

"Never mind that bravado front he puts on..." said Willie slowly shaking his head from side to side.

It was all coming together now. I thought of the time recently when Todd almost blew my head off after I asked him about his search for a teaching position. Now I understood why. I felt his pain.

"So are all the young black men going to be harassed by the police now?" asked Jessica looking nervously in the direction of her son Joshua, who fit the description of 'black' and 'tall' very well.

"They'd better not," said Jolene calmly. She had just completed a law degree following in her father's footsteps. She was a bright, astute young woman. I had a feeling that some day she would be quite a formidable force. And we needed it!

As soon as I arrived home I called Tiffany. I'd been busy the entire weekend and had not spoken to her. Ayanna wanted to know when she was coming over for another visit. Tiffany had told her about the school concert in which she was singing a solo and Ayanna was planning to attend. So at the risk of getting her mother all riled up I picked up the receiver. The familiar buzzing sound informed me that there was a call in my voice mail, which I decided to take before calling Tiffany. "Aunt Bon..." It was definitely Tiffany's voice that for some reason was aborted in mid-sentence. I dialed their number. There was no answer.

    I called Adlyn. We chatted about the folks that were now on their way back to Toronto. Curt had volunteered to travel in Todd's car to keep him company, Ad said. I could tell that the delight and excitement of the party were diminished by what happened to Todd later on. I had a creepy feeling about the stranger I'd met in the park and told Ad all about the encounter. I wondered whether I should report it to the police, but Ad advised me against this. "They'll probably turn it back on you," she said. "Try to link you with the stabber." Especially as the police were looking for someone fitting Todd's description. I sighed. It probably wouldn't be of any use.

    "Got to go now," I said to Ad. "I want to get Tiffany before she goes to bed."

"All day long me been tryin' to get Reg," said Ad jolting me. "An' nobody home."
Was something the matter with Regina and/or Tiffany?

I got Michael's call after midnight. He sounded tired but insisted that he was very well. "I guess now I have a woman like you, it feels like I'm wasting my time here," he told me. "I can't wait to get back to you, my darling." My heart sang with joy and I responded with much of the same. I longed for the feel of his arms around me. Skipping over unpleasant stuff like the stabbing in the park, I gave him all the good news of Ad and Herbert's party. "It's going to be a great restaurant," I told him. "And that's the first place we're going to go, when you come home."

"Was Regina at the party?" he asked me directly.

"No."

"How is Tiffany? Did you see her this weekend?" Michael had a way of cutting through red tape and getting straight to the point.

"I called Tiffany earlier tonight but I guess she and her Mum were out..."

"Boni... could you please find out what's going on for me?"

"Eh?"

"I've been calling since yesterday and when I couldn't get them I finally called the management of the building. I was told that apartment is now vacant."

"Vacant?... but that can't be... where are they?" Did I hear Michael correctly?

"I don't know... but Boni... could you please look out for Tiffany for me..."

"Of course... I'll try to find out where they are..."

"Thanks my darling... I don't know what I'd do without you. You are my sustenance... my life line."
My mind was becoming fuzzy. Days later I would learn what had actually happened to Tiffany.

Tiffany had arrived home from school on Friday evening to find that the lock to their apartment door had been changed. After trying over and over to unlock the door, she decided to look for the janitor. However, as she got out of the elevator on the ground level, Regina was waiting for her in the lobby.

"Mum," Tiffany shouted happy to see her mother who would now be able to fix the problem with the door. "Something's wrong with my key... I can't open the door."

"Shhh...," said Regina. "Come with me."
Walking quickly, Regina led her out of the building and they headed towards the parking lot.

"Where're we going to Mum?" asked Tiffany.

"We don't live here anymore," answered Regina.
Tiffany was stunned. "Whaat? Why not Mum?" Looking at her mother's face, she knew it was not a good idea to question her too much. Without answering, Regina led her to the parking lot, where McIvor, with cigarette lit, was waiting in his car for them.

"Get in," said Regina opening the back door of the car. Tiffany obeyed.

"Hello," said McIvor. He was a man of few words where children were concerned.

They drove in silence for what seemed a long time to Tiffany, until they came to the development where McIvor lived. Her mother led her into his house, which although grand looking from the outside was cold and shabby within. They went down a hallway into a small bedroom, with stained carpets. The coverlet on the bed had a musty scent and was dark coloured, probably to hide dirt, Tiffany suspected. She noticed that there were suitcases and boxes randomly dumped about the room.

"We're going to be staying here for a while," said Regina. "Your clothes and other stuff are in these." She waved her arm at the boxes and suitcases.

"What? Why we staying here?" asked Tiffany.

"Tiffany, you don't know how very lucky we are to have a place like this to live."

"But why can't we live at the Southpark apartments... it's so close to school... and to Aunt Boni's apartment."

"You won't be going back to that school," answered Regina.

"Whaat? I'm not going back to my school?" Tiffany began to cry now. These words from Regina had a devastating impact on her.

"There's a school just down the street here, that I'm going to switch you to," said Regina. "It'll be okay darling." She placed her arms around Tiffany, but Tiffany was inconsolable.

"It's not okay Mum. I can't change schools Mum," said Tiffany turning to look at Regina directly eye to eye. "It's the middle of the term and besides I'm in the school concert."

"We don't have a choice," answered Regina sitting wearily down on the bed.

Tiffany wasn't buying any of this. "I can't switch schools now Mum" she repeated. "They chose me as the soloist in the Christmas concert." She had been hoping to surprise her Mum with this.

"I'm sorry, but since I can't afford Southpark any longer and since..." Regina seemed at a lost for words. She did not comment on her daughter's part in the school concert.

"I'm sure I can stay with Aunt Boni..."

"Please be reasonable Tiffany..."

"You're the one that's unreasonable Mum..." said Tiffany harshly.

Regina got up from the bed. "If you're going to be rude, I don't have anything more to say to you." She stormed out of the room. Tiffany threw herself across the bed, forgetting the dirt she suspected was on the coverlet, and drained and exhausted cried herself to sleep.

She awoke much later with hunger pangs propelling her out of bed. She urgently needed to talk to her dad and to Aunt Boni. She heard voices from the living room and went to investigate. On the way she made a stop in a dingy bathroom with a strong medicinal scent.

She peeped at Regina and McIvor in the living room. They both huddled seriously over forms and cards that were laid out on the living room table. The room was stuffy with cigarette smoke causing Tiffany's eyes to burn.

"Can't you get her father to help?"

"I've already asked him..."

"Well, it's his child too..."

"But most of these costs don't have anything to do with Tiffany," said Regina as with a pencil she pointed to a form they were looking at.

"Never mind... you can't separate them out..."

Regina mumbled something, which Tiffany didn't quite hear, at the same time as she looked up and saw Tiffany standing in the doorway.

"Hi Tiff, do you want some pizza?" she asked, pointing to the dining room table, where a big pizza box lay.

"Had an early sleep, eh?" said McIvor as he grinned at her.

Without answering, Tiffany sat slowly down at the dining room table and began to eat the slices of pizza, now cold, that had been left in the box. A can of coke was left beside the pizza for her. I've got to call Aunt Boni, she thought to herself, as she chewed the hard pizza crust. But there was no visible phone in the usual places - living/dining room, kitchen.

"Tiffany, tomorrow before I go to work, we have an appointment with the principal of the school you'll be attending on Monday... she's making special time for us," said Regina as getting up from the sofa she walked towards the dining room table and took a seat opposite Tiffany. With his feet resting on the coffee table, McIvor puffed at a freshly lit cigarette.

"Mum... I'm not going to any new school on Monday...I already told you so."

"Tiffany, please stop being difficult." Regina's voice was soft but strident. It had that unmistakable timbre of one on the verge of tears. "I already have more on my plate than I could cope with."

Just then McIvor answered his cellular phone, which he kept in the pocket of his trousers.

"Can I borrow that phone please?" Tiffany asked him, when he was finished.

"What for?" demanded Regina.

"I want to call Aunt Boni," said Tiffany being very straight forward and up front.

"I don't want you telling anyone my business," answered Regina, her voice louder this time.

"Sorry but there's no more time left on it," said McIvor. "I've got to purchase some more time."

Tiffany didn't believe him one bit but she caught a glimpse of the plan. She knew she had to get hold of Aunt Boni as soon as she got an opportunity.

19

Sitting in the audience with me the day of the Christmas concert at Tiffany's school were Madge and Ayanna. Madge and her family were planning to spend Christmas in Toronto with Fleurina and despite the demands on her time that the season imposed, she'd made a special effort to attend and show support for Tiffany. As to be expected, most of Adlyn's spare time was now taken up helping Herbert in the restaurant, so she wasn't able to attend. Michael, unfortunately couldn't be back in time for the concert and now Christmas was looking 'iffy'. After all the commotion a few weeks ago, I didn't expect to see Regina.

Regina was in severe financial straits and had been evicted from her apartment. She had filed for bankruptcy protection and she and McIvor were currently taking refuge in his mother's home in Casowick - a community west of Ottawa. His mother was one of those 'snowbirds' who wintered in Florida every year. She was not expected back before May.

Regina had managed yet another time in her life to 'max out' her credit cards. Her car and most of her new furniture had been repossessed. I gathered that McIvor, twice divorced and probably paying alimony and child support, was also living on the edge. The hope of a windfall at the casino, where complementary drinks and snacks floated by, far from helping, just compounded the problem.

I recalled my arrival at the clinic on that memorable Monday morning, with a million pressing issues competing unrelentlessly for my attention. Foremost among them was Tiffany. I had to find out what was going on with her and Regina. Why were they no longer at the Southpark apartment and where were they. When Michael called I could sense his distress at the situation, which was the last thing he needed at that time. I decided to start with Adlyn. She might have some information on how to contact McIvor, who would no doubt know where Regina and Tiffany were.

Before I could speak to Adlyn, I received a surprise call from Michael himself. He never called me at work. He had spoken to Regina at her workplace, and found out where they were and some of what was going on. I don't know what magic buttons he pushed or pulled; I knew he must have done some 'fancy footwork' because Regina agreed to allow Tiffany to stay with me. I was to pick her up that night.

"Boni...you are my lifeline," he said to me more than once.

On the heels of that call, a very distressed Tiffany phoned me from the school in Casowick. Poor child, she had tried to get me before but McIvor's cell phone had gone blank. When she heard that her father had made arrangements for me to pick her up that night, she could hardly contain herself.

"I'll be over as soon as I'm finished with work," I assured her.

I left work promptly that day but not before checking on the progress of the young lady who had been stabbed in the park last Friday night. The news was positive. She was still in ICU but her prognosis was good. She was extremely lucky to have survived as the knife had passed within an inch of her heart. Somehow I felt a certain kinship with this unknown woman.

Contrary to predictions of yesterday's weather forecast, freezing rain had fallen in the city making the driving slow and hazardous; then there was an accident on the Queensway backing up traffic to a crawl for miles. I was counting the minutes and praying that I could get Tiffany away before Regina and McIvor arrived home. I had an instinctive feeling that they would try to put a spoke in our wheels, regardless of what agreement Regina had reached with Michael.

Finally much later than I had intended, I arrived at the house in Casowick, equipped with a fax from Michael with Regina's signature agreeing to let Tiffany into my care. Thankfully Regina and McIvor had not yet arrived home. Tiffany was waiting impatiently for me. We hastened to load my car with her belongings, which had remained in their suitcases and boxes, unpacked, in the room she stayed. She left a note on the dining table for her mother and returned the house key to its hiding place in a flowerpot.

As we turned the corner on to Casowick street, stopped at the traffic lights was McIvor's green *Volvo*. I hoped they didn't notice us. We had gotten away by the skin of our teeth.

"Penny for your thoughts, girl," said Madge smiling at me.

"I'm so sorry" I said, embarrassed to be caught daydreaming. "It's so good of y'all to come out for Tiffany." The principal of the school had been talking but Lord knows I hadn't heard a single word she'd said.

"It's going to start now," said Ayanna excitedly.

In the final act, Tiffany had both a solo and a duet. She sang beautifully. I think we were all amazed at the expressiveness and control of her voice. I thought I could identify some influences from the gospel choir we had attended in Montreal last October. Hopefully our cheers, loudly added to the enthusiastic ovation from the audience, made up for the absence of her parents.

Tiffany and I had a quiet but happy Christmas together. She spent part of the day skating on the Rideau canal with some of her friends from the Christmas concert. I'd given up my initial plan to spend the holidays sorting all the junk in my apartment, shredding old documents and planning the purchasing of necessary items for my new townhouse. Instead, since Tiffany was with me, I decided to give my apartment a festive aura. We purchased a small tree, which we had great fun picking out, and went a bit wild with the decorations, but it was lots of crazy, happy fun.

While the turkey was in the oven, I made my usual call to Mother on Christmas morning. Brenda was visiting so I was able to wish them both holiday greetings and between the two of them I was filled in on the goings-on at home.

I had just missed Stonehead who'd returned to England the day before. Unlike Lucille, after Uncle Nat's funeral he had stayed on for MLP's wedding.

"If she'd a' answer the phone you wudda hear a loud 'Hello... Mrs. Sylvester speakin'," said Brenda as she gave her loud 'fish woman' laugh which ended with a high pitched "eeeyeee!" "You cyan' call the woman no MLP anymore. She's a highfalutin Mrs. Sylvester now if you please."

I laughed along with Brenda. "How did the wedding go?" I asked.

"Well she got her long white veil held up by her entourage of brides maids, all her children."

MLP, age and children notwithstanding, had wanted all the bells and whistles for her wedding, but I gathered Aunt Sybil's practicality had prevailed.

"We don' have no money to spen' on big weddin'...what yoh want all dat stupidness for?" or "yoh cyan' have no veil over yoh face gyurl, wid yoh belly stickin' out like dat." Aunt Sybil had been firm. Eventually they'd had a small but fine ceremony in the St. George's cathedral and the classy reception held at Mother's place consisted of family and close friends.

Stonehead, now a physician, was planning to return to set up practice in Grenada in partnership with two other doctors, said Mother. He was encouraging Brenda to join the staff at the clinic. "It so good dat not everybody turn dey back on dey homeland," she added pointedly. I ignored that comment.

"And what's Mr. Sylvester like?" Brenda had told me that that was how Patty and the children referred to him.

"The Vincee? Not bad... he very hard working," admitted Brenda. "You know he does some carpentry and stonemason work... so he busy down at the medical school now."

"He pleasant enough," added Mother.

I gathered Mr. Sylvester had passed the test.

I inquired about Lucille, recently a co-owner of a beauty salon in California. She had taken MLP's two eldest daughters to live with her in California.

"De girls come for de wedding," said Mother. "But Lucille say she had to go back for her work."

"You'll see de pictures," stated Brenda. "Everyone lookin' real spiffy."

No sooner had I hung up the receiver than another call, long distance, was coming in.

"Hello," I crooned into the receiver, using the voice I reserved for Michael.

"BeeBee Merry Christmas!"

I tried not to sound too disappointed. "Todd... Merry Christmas... how are you? It's so nice hearing from you," I blurted out all at once. We had been chatting for a while when Todd told me he was moving soon to Alberta. "There's nothing for me here BeeBee," he concluded. I was truly sorry for what he'd gone through and it was from the bottom of my heart that I wished him God's speed and all the best.

I was talking to Madge and Fleurina in Toronto when Tiffany returned, red faced but happy, from skating on the Rideau canal. Jessica and family as well as their brother and his family were all going over later to Flo's place for Christmas dinner.

"Daddy?" Tiffany mimed and I shook my head negatively. However since Ayanna had inquired about Tiffany, I let them say a few words to each other.

Both Ad and Herbie were exhausted after a very hectic Christmas eve at the restaurant. With Sharon opting to spend the holidays with her mother in Toronto, they allowed themselves the luxury of a Christmas day in bed and gently declined my offer of Christmas dinner. The life of a new entrepreneur was proving to be very hectic.

There was no call from Regina or Michael that Christmas day. I felt sorry for Tiffany and tried my best to make it up to her. Each time the phone rang, she looked at it expectantly. For yet another important time in her life, neither parent was there for her. No calls either.

20

Early in the New Year, after almost a three-week blackout, we received Michael's call from a military hospital in Germany. He'd been wounded in the shoulder he said and had been transported there.

Tiffany and I were relieved as well as ecstatic. Although I hadn't said anything to her, I had secretly been fearing the worst. It was not like Michael to remain silent for so long. I confided in Fleurina and Madge who gave me much moral support during that time. These women had replaced Regina and to some extent Adlyn as my confidantes.

Sometimes out of darkness comes the light as Michael's injury had spearheaded an honourable discharge from a fifteen year career in the military. He was returning to Canada in approximately one month. But I kept my optimism to myself. Canadian forces were currently deployed not only to support peacekeeping efforts in the wars of the Yugoslav succession, but there were ongoing missions in the Persian Gulf as well as other regions of conflict throughout the world in which they participated. He had done his part and I was happy he was coming home. With renewed vim and vigour Tiffany and I went about our daily activities appreciating those special blessings in our lives.

Michael resumed his calls to us as often as he could. He was disappointed to have missed Tiffany's school concert. He was happy that we had a good Christmas and regretted not having been there with us. Tiffany's eyes sparkled with pride as she told her father that she had made the honour roll at school and that even Mrs. Howard was being nice to her. She related to him all the details of the school concert, which had been a great success. Yes, she was nervous at first, she admitted to him, but that just melted away as soon as she started to sing. He also learned the progress of my new home, which I was moving into at the beginning of March and those fun shopping trips to furniture stores that Tiffany and I had been making.

The only fly in the ointment was concerning Regina, from whom neither of us had heard a single word in weeks. If the truth be known, I secretly missed having Regina's advice with the decoration of my townhouse. She did have a knack for coordination.

"Regina seems to have an empty hole that has to be filled by excessive shopping or gambling," Michael said to me one night when Tiffany was not also on the line.

I remembered the fancy, expensive hotel room in Toronto we had checked into, her trip to Vegas, her brand new furniture, and other expensive items and I said, "She always seems to spend money so freely..."

"Yes... all her new furniture was bought on credit cards from three different stores."

"Good God!" I exclaimed.

"We'd been down that road before," continued Michael. "She is well aware that the interest starts accruing from the date of purchase... and sometimes it can be a whopping 25%."

"Yes... credit card debt can certainly sink you fast."

"Like I said we were down that road before...Regina knows that."

"Perhaps she was influenced by her new beau."

"I'm so glad that Tiffany is no longer with her," said Michael ignoring the reference to Regina's new beau. "Actually I was pleasantly surprised when she allowed Tiffany to go with you that easily."

I began to tell him about our narrow escape from McIvor's home in Casowick that Monday, just as someone on the other end was trying to get his attention.

"Excuse me," Michael said to me and I could hear him speaking to someone in the background. "Sweetheart, I've got to have my bandages changed now... so until tomorrow night... bye."

We blew kisses at each other through the phone. There were so many things I wanted to discuss with him but because of his trauma, I was being extra cautious.

It was a spur of the moment decision and I'm not given to many of those. On my way home from work, I decided to visit the local police precinct. A composite sketch of the park stabber had been appearing on every local newscast and it bore no resemblance to the guy that I'd bumped into that night in Ainsley Park. So against the advice of Ad and Herbert, I decided to do my civic duty. I would provide them with a description of the guy I'd seen and if it helped... good. If it didn't... well, I didn't see how it could possibly do any harm.

In that I was mistaken. Looking at me suspiciously, the policeman who heard my statement wondered why it took such a long time for me to make this report. I felt on the defensive.

"It's not as though I've got a lot of spare time on my hands," I answered. It bothered me that most of the questions asked were personal questions about me. Where did I work, what did I do, for how long. My ID was requested and checked. I was relieved to hightail it out of that place. Maybe my coming in with this information now was going to upset the apple cart? Maybe they were closing in on somebody and didn't want to be told they were wrong? I didn't know. However the deed was done and was it correct? I didn't know.

The delicious smell of black-eyed peas simmering with salted pigs' tails soothed my tattered nerves as I arrived home that evening. This is one of the dishes Tiffany and I both loved and after a gloomy winter's day combined with my regrettable visit to the police precinct, I felt I could certainly do with some comfort food. Tiffany was becoming quite proficient in the kitchen and I encouraged her to cook most meals rather than rely on 'take out'. She was planning on making this dish for her dad when he returned she said, as we sat down for supper that evening.

"Meeting, meeting, meeting..." droned Mason as he scurried behind the desk for a pencil and notepad, to take off to a meeting in the auditorium. The few long strands of his hair that he thought concealed his bald spot had stubbornly opted to stand at attention. Mason constantly complained about all the committees he was required to sit on, with meetings every week. He thought many of them were pointless and dug into that precious commodity - time. I personally believed that sometimes he didn't mind one bit leaving the unit behind and going somewhere else for a breather.

As he was about to step out, the phone rang for him.

"Mason, it's the lab for you. Can you take it?" asked Francine.

"Mais non. C'est n'est pas possible" answered Mason pouting his face as though he wanted to cry while at the same time looking in my direction.

"I'll take care of it," I answered as I waved him off to his meeting. He was gone in a flash.

"Mason's at a meeting... Boni Burke here... can I help you?" I said into the phone. Yikes, it was the transfusion manager. Had I known it was her, I would not have been so generous to Mason.

"Miss Burke... we have a problem."

"Yes... what is it?"

"The lab just received a specimen from a patient with the name Jacqueline Dacota, which tested O Neg."

"Yes?" The ditch lady was in again, I thought. The transfusion manager continued. "The problem is this patient came in through your clinic last October..."
Since when did the clinic become mine, I wondered. This lady had a way of pressing my damn buttons.

"She had a hysterectomy and her specimen was A Positive then," stated the transfusion manager.
I almost dropped the phone. "Is that right?" I remembered every detail of the 'ditch lady's' face.

"Yes... we've repeated the test with a new specimen."

I was dumbfounded. "And what did the repeat specimen show?"

"The same results... O Negative. So something is definitely wrong and I'm going to initiate an incident report. We have to investigate."

I agreed. There were two different blood groups for the same patient. The ID was identical but was it the same patient?

I don't know why I chose to return from my lunch break via the stairs rather than the escalator the following day. But ahead of me on the stairs I heard Francine's voice complaining to someone.

"Yes, she must have mixed up the patient's ID," she stated. "It's obvious that these are two different patients."

"Yes?"

"Dr. Hendricks checked on the patient this morning and there were no surgical scars, nothing..."

"And she had a hysterectomy last October? Perhaps this lady is using someone else's ID," suggested the person she was speaking to.

"Or perhaps she mixed up the ID..."

"That could be..."

"I'm watching to see if they're going to promote her when Mason leaves...with all those mistakes she's been making recently."

"Yes?"

"You remember that patient she almost killed with the preservative?"

I hesitated. Francine didn't actually call my name but it was obvious that the person she was referring to was me. I was disgusted. She had me signed, sealed and delivered already. Without letting my presence be known, like a ghost I quietly slipped out of the stairwell.

Silently stewing from what I considered Francine's betrayal, I decided to do my own little investigation and paid Mrs. Dacota a visit on the ward. Sitting up in her bed answering questions from a young resident was a bespectacled, dark-haired, long-faced woman. There was no 'bird crap' mark on her forehead. This was not the ditch lady. This was not Mrs. Dacota. If she was, then the previous lady - my lady of the ditch - had falsely used her ID.

"Do you have a friend with a darkened birthmark on her forehead?" I asked this lady after I had introduced myself to her and the resident. The way she coughed and sputtered and stammered convinced me and the resident present that I was on to something.

"Nooo," she replied hesitantly.

"She has a foreign accent and a little boy about five or six years old," I encouraged her.

Surprised at how much I knew, the woman must have thought a clairvoyant had been brought in. Looking at me curiously she added after a while as though just recalling that fact, "I think my next door neighbour has a birthmark on her forehead... and yes I think she has a little boy."

"Do you know if she had surgery here last October?"

The woman looked very uncomfortable. She held her head down. "I think so," she replied.

I felt like Agatha Christie's Hercule Poirot.

"That's the woman who used your ID last October," I said. "Do you know how she got it?"

"Nooo," replied the patient unconvincingly. Whether or not these women were friends we could never be sure. They certainly had no inkling that their deception would be discovered and how dangerous it could be.

The investigative report was finalized a few weeks later. Mason read it to both myself and Francine as we huddled around his desk. The report concluded that the second patient, who produced other ID to confirm that fact, was indeed Jacqueline Dacota. The first woman who had a hysterectomy in October and who tested A Positive, could have fraudulently used the same ID. Thanks to the superb skills of Boni Burke, a note was made of important distinguishing characteristics of this first patient.

"Good work Boni," said Mason with exuberance putting his hand up to slap high five with me. "*Felicitacions.*"

"Good for you Boni," said Francine as with cold eyes she bared her picket line of tiny, too perfectly shaped teeth at me.

This year I applied to take one of my vacation weeks to coincide with my moving date and since Mason and Francine usually took the months of July and August off respectively, I decided to reserve the last two weeks in June to take Mother and Brenda around, which left me with another week I could take in one day segments from time to time especially around long weekends.

It was two weekends before my move and I was buried deep into packing and sorting and discarding. Tiffany spent a lot of her time on weekends with Ayanna or Carole, her school friend from the Christmas concert, with whom she went skating occasionally. Last weekend she traveled to Toronto with the Johnsons. They stayed with Fleurina and her family. Today she went skating with Carole. I encouraged her to get some physical exercise by doing something she enjoyed. When she returned to her mother's fare of chips and sugary soft drinks in abundance she regained the pounds she had lost. Knowing that the medical community was seeing a rise in the incidence of juvenile diabetes, I encouraged Tiffany to cut down on refined foods as well as pursue a physical activity she enjoyed.

In the meantime I anxiously awaited Michael's call to let me know the exact details of his flight the following week. Finally around three o' clock that Saturday he called.

"Are you going out this evening?" he asked me.

"Going out? I'm neck deep in packing my stuff," I laughed. "Anyhow...why don't you let me have your flight number and time..."

"I haven't received all those details yet, but I'll let you have them as soon as I do."

"Not yet?" I couldn't believe my ears. What was the matter with this guy? A week before his travel and he didn't have that information yet. I sighed.

"What's the matter honey?"

"I think you're leaving everything till the last minute..." I didn't want to come down on him like a ton of bricks but I wanted to light a fire in his backside.

"Don't worry about that darling." He brushed aside my concerns. "Anyhow did you receive my last cheque for Tiffany?"

"Yes I received it," I answered.

"I'll make up the rest to you as soon as I can." He had previously hinted that he was having to dole out a tidy sum to Regina - the price he had to pay for 'freeing' Tiffany.

"Don't worry about that." I thought I'd use his exact words back at him. "I wish you'd worry instead about getting your travel details together." I was getting tired. First he was coming home for Tiffany's concert, then it slipped to Christmas, then he was coming in one month, then now the middle of February, he still could not give me exact details of his travel arrangements. My oozing heart felt like it was about to dry up.

At about six o' clock the buzzer sounded. Who the hell was that, I wondered as I looked at Tiffany, who'd come in from skating a little while ago.

"Did Daddy call?" had been the first words out her mouth as she stepped into the apartment.

"Yes, he did about two hours ago," I answered.

"Yippee!" she exclaimed. She seemed so upbeat.

"But he still can't tell me his travel plans," I continued rather petulantly. Tiffany planted a loud kiss on my cheek, perhaps to console me as she bounced into the bedroom to place an order for pizza delivery.

"Are you expecting anyone? It can't be the pizza already," I said to Tiffany now from the kitchen.

"I think it is," she replied as going to the area by the door she buzzed the pizza man in but returned to her bedroom to get the money for the pizza, I assumed.

Dressed in an old sweat suit with a dust rag tying my head, I left my packing to answer the knock at the door a few moments later. I blinked. This wasn't the pizza man. I couldn't believe my eyes. I remained frozen as I stood in the doorway gaping.

21

"Daddy! Daddy!" shouted Tiffany as she pushed past me and hugged and pulled a smiling Michael into my apartment.

"Give me some love, girl" he said to me putting down his bag, when Tiffany had released him. With one arm he embraced me. The other arm was still in a sling. My knees weakened. My heart was somersaulting. "Don't punish me for lying to you today girl. Give me some love."

"O God! Honey, is it really you?" I asked as I gathered him into my arms and kissed him.

"In the flesh," he smiled looking at me with those deep, dark eyes of his.

"But I thought you were calling me from Germany this afternoon..." I was still hugging him and now Tiffany joined the huddle.

"No...I'd just landed at Mirabel airport. I took a taxi and came here as soon as I could."

"You took a taxi from Mirabel? But why you didn't let me come to pick you up?"

"Don't worry... that's part of my severance perks," he replied as he kissed our foreheads ever so gently.

So Tiffany had been in the loop. Michael had told her he was coming on Saturday and wanted to surprise me. He'd promised he would call as soon as he landed at Mirabel. That's why Tiffany was so exuberant when I told her he'd called two hours ago. She knew he was on his way.

Michael had arranged for the rental of an apartment in the same Southpark complex where Tiffany used to live. He chose there because of its proximity to her school.

We sat around my coffee table eating pizza - Roman's pizza was Michael's favorite fast food meal - and drinking wine. I'd changed from my old sweats into something more presentable for Michael. "You're beautiful no matter what you're in," he'd said and my heart wanted to burst with happiness when he put his arms around me and said "Boni, you are my lifeline." Softly in my ear he whispered, "Your love is like an invisible tube that feeds me, that sustains me no matter how far away we may be from each other." He had lost some weight. I could tell the last few months had been hard on him. I looked at his wound which although nicely healed now must have been quite significant. The doctors still wanted him to use a sling for a while longer.

At church the next morning, I thanked the Lord for being gracious unto us. "Peace be with you," I wished Michael and Tiffany and others sitting in pews next to us from the very bottom of my heart. Despite the dark, cold weather and having gone to bed very late the night before, neither Michael nor Tiffany resisted when I woke them up to go to church early the next morning. We even had to make a short stop off for a change of clothes at the Southpark apartment, where Michael had left his luggage.

It seemed like I clicked my fingers and the next few weeks just flew by. Michael and Tiffany moved into the Southpark apartment and I moved into my new home. Michael's furniture, which had been in storage in Montreal, was delivered to his apartment. Without too many mess ups, appliances as well as the living room and bedroom furniture I had checked out with Tiffany and later purchased were delivered to my townhouse.

On the down side we learned that Regina was going through a dark period of depression and had been off work for a few weeks. I encouraged Michael and Tiffany to visit her but I thought my own presence - that of ex best friend - might not be very helpful to her at this time.

At the end of my week off from work, I kept my promise and took Michael to *The Caribbean Kitchen*. It was time now for us to come out of the closet regarding our relationship, I thought.

"You t'ink you been foolin' anybody?" said Ad as she gathered us both in a strong embrace, while Herbie stood by with a big grin on his face. "Me done smell a rat long time."

As I expected, we both enjoyed our meals tremendously. Running a restaurant was hard work but Ad and Herbie were weathering the storms. Ad complained that a lot of her 'yard' people seemed to like to hang around the restaurant. She tried to dissuade them but since they supported the restaurant, it was quite a balancing act. "It's bad for business," she said and I agreed. On her agenda once the restaurant was well established and running smoothly, she said, was to open a games room nearby for them to hang out.

As expected, back at my home later, Michael and I settled down to enjoy the rest of the evening together. Tiffany was spending the weekend with Ayanna. What I did not expect was the diamond ring Michael produced from a little box in the breast pocket of his shirt and his formal proposal of marriage to me.

As though from a distant land bells of happiness sounded, concentrating its gentle tolls in the centre of my own being, as I gladly accepted to spend the rest of my life with this man. Together we would find jubilation, together we would make music, lulling to a sleepy vale any discordant notes that threatened to prevail. It was like the sun upon a snowy terrain, shining upon silver sparkles that leap forth from amidst the white. I wanted to jump with joy, to announce to the world, to mother, sister, friend or foe that a love, pure and absolute was about to grow.

Tiffany was overjoyed when she learned that the three of us were going to become a family unit. In case she felt she was being disloyal to her mother, I sat down with her and assured her I could never replace her own mother in her life. "She'll always be your mother," I said. "And I'd like to continue to be your Aunt Boni."

"Love is not like a pie," her father said to her. "That if you give a big slice to someone, there's less for another." Tiffany and I both looked at Michael. "Consider it a magic dish," he continued. "It's bottomless. The more you scoop, the more there is to be scooped. There is no end."

Ad and Herbie were disappointed that Michael did not pop the question while at the restaurant. "We would a' open de special champagne to toast unnu wid," Ad said and I knew that fuss and publicity was exactly what Michael wished to avoid.

The following week I received a lovely handmade card of congratulations from Sharon. I was touched by the words which stated that I was one of her favorite persons and she wished me all the happiness in the world. She said she would be happy to decorate the church and reception hall for us if we so desired.

Fleurina, Madge, Jessica and their families were thrilled when they heard the news.

"I'll be honoured to make your wedding gown," said Flo when I wondered aloud whether I could employ her skills in that department.

Mother and Brenda were wild with excitement. "I hope y'all planning to tie the knot while we up there," said Mother. Michael and I had not given a single thought to date or place yet.

Michael got his own mother on the phone from Barbados and we spoke briefly. Even though we didn't know each other, I found her sincere.

"All I want is my son's happiness," she said. "And he seems so happy with you."

Even Veronique in Montreal called to express her joy for us. "You are a strong woman," she said to me. "Comfortable in your own skin... but thank God Michael is not one of those men who feel threatened by that quality."

"Yes?" I thought Veronique was very much a strong woman herself, quite an asset for someone raising two teenagers alone and from all reports being very successful. But was that the quality that made her husband flee for a 'softer' version? Historically many black women have had to be strong, donning a mask of toughness necessary for survival. Veronique's ex-husband used to complain of 'too much lip' or 'drama' or that she was not being sufficiently supportive - code I think for not mildly accepting whatever crap came flying at her.

"It do me heart good to know dat Michael fin' a good, strong woman like you," said Veronique seriously, returning to her patois.

"Thanks Veronique," I replied slightly embarrassed by her fervour. But I knew what she was referring to.

22

"Welcome to Canada," I said to Mother and Brenda as they arrived in Ottawa one cold night in March. We all embraced warmly and kissed each other. They were bundled up like two onions, heeding my persistent warning that this cold weather was nothing to fool around with. From my sports bag I supplied them with the necessary winter gear, some of which were donated from Ad's closets.

"If I knew this place was so damn cold, I wouldn't a' come now," said Mother.

"Yes... why you didn't tell us how cold this place was?" added Brenda with a twinkle in her eyes.
I had been careful to mention that fact to both of them many, many times.

"Let me see your ring, girl" said Brenda reaching for my left hand. "Nice," she said referring both to my ring and my professionally manicured nails, which I'd recently treated myself to.

"So when we gwine meet Michael?" asked Mother.

"Tomorrow," I replied. "After work tomorrow. He started a new job today."

"That's right... you said he's no longer with the armed forces."

I left them waiting with their luggage to go warm up my car and drive it from the parking lot to the door of the terminal.

"I believe you guys hiding some dead bodies in here," I joked as I hoisted the heavy bags into the trunk of my car, careful not to break my nails.

Back at home, after we'd lugged the bags up the stairs to the bedrooms they were going to occupy, and after they'd changed into more comfortable attire, we settled down to the meal I'd spent the better part of the day preparing.

"Cheers for a great holiday!" I said as I held my wine glass aloft after we'd said grace before meals. I was still standing.

"Cheers!" replied Brenda.

"My God Bunny," said Mother noticing me without my coat for the first time. "You get so thin. What happenin' to you?"

I had been proud of the pounds I'd dropped and of the fact that I was now a svelte size 10. Now through my mother's eyes I looked thin and sick. "Nothing Mother ... I've been exercising and trimming down," I answered as I swung around to show off my trim, new figure.

Mother frowned and pursed her lips. "Girl... where yoh bambam gone? An' where yoh breast hidin'?"

I looked at Brenda for help. She'd always been the slim one, while I was the one with the 'good' figure - big breasted with a big backside. Now I was even slimmer than Brenda.

Mother continued. "Dis bag o' bones Twiggy figure, dat everybody say nice... let me tell you something nuh... it damn ugly."

"Mother, I'm far from being Twiggy," I objected irritably.

"You use to have a nice woman-figure, Bunny... childbearing hips and nice big tits... but you had to go get rid o' it." She steupsed loudly.

Brenda gave me a look which said, "See why I had to move out on my own?"

We began the meal in relative quiet. I was inwardly seething. Brenda broke the silence by telling me how well Clyde was doing. Thanks to Stonehead he'd had surgery on his deformed, crippled legs and had been fitted with prostheses which he was gradually getting used to. "It's great to see him standing upright now and I think it's doing wonders for his self image." She was obviously very impressed with Stonehead, and revealed her plan to work with him in the clinic he was planning to set up when he returned to Grenada. Again, I expressed my sorrow that I hadn't seen him or Lucille, in over fifteen years.

Lucille and Stonehead went to England the year after I left Grenada. In typical tradition Lucille became a nurse but left for the U.S. shortly after. She settled in California, where after a few years as a nurse she returned to school to study cosmetology. That was where her passion lay, she explained to her querulous parents. She later expanded a hairdressing salon in which she had bought shares, to include facials, manicures and pedicures. Having more work than she could cope with, and seeing the possibility of further expansion, she recruited Mavis and Gladys, MLP's first two daughters, who jumped at the idea of going to California and broadening their horizons. All reports to date indicated that business was doing well and all were fine.

    I never understood why Clyde did not resent me. I was the cousin who took Lucille and Stonehead away from him; monopolized their time whenever I visited. His deformity prevented him from attending school, his parents needlessly fearing the cruelty he may have been subjected to by school children. Nevertheless he achieved a high level of literacy, siphoned off no doubt from his younger siblings. I think he appreciated the comic books and the stories, slightly embellished, of life in St. George's I brought him from time to time. In return I was treated to hair-raising stories of *La Diablesse* and *Loupgarou* - a nocturnal vampire. I was happy to hear that the quality of Clyde's life was about to improve.

    When Brenda described MLP's recent obsession with speaking proper English, it was difficult for me to keep a straight face. In keeping with her elevated status as married woman, MLP tried not to use the dialect anymore and was constantly admonishing her children to speak properly. In a nice, clear voice she said to Brenda one day, "Where does you works in St. George's Brenda?" I had no choice but to crack up.

    After we'd cleaned up following the meal, Mother and Brenda showed themselves around my little three-bedroom home.

    "Is a beautiful place you have here," said Mother. "And I love yoh livin' room furniture." I was finally getting a compliment from my mother. "I really like how yoh done de drapes," she continued earnestly, making me drop the peevishness I'd been feeling towards her.

They brought me a letter from MLP which was cute. It included a few of her wedding pictures for me. She congratulated me on my engagement and offered to give me her expert advice anytime, she being the "fust to married." I was surprised at how grownup many of the children were, especially her two eldest girls.

"Dey look jus' like dey father," said Mother.

"Their father? I don't know their father."

"Sure you do," answered Mother. "Is Aunt Theresa's brother."

I didn't need a DNA test to confirm the truth of what Mother said. Those young ladies were the spitting image of their father - a married gentleman, considered respectable and at least thirty years Patty's senior. Patty was a young girl about fifteen years old when she had her first baby. I realized that was probably the reason her mother, Aunt Sybil, refused to have anything to do with anyone in that family including Aunt Theresa. I felt sympathy for MLP, whom I thought had been taken advantage of by a grown man. I regretted participating in all those awful jokes, in which we referred to Patty as a clothes pin - you squeeze the head and the legs open - and I resolved to call her MLP no longer.

Nanny once told me that Aunt Theresa boasted that her great grandfather used to be a governor in Grenada. Whether this was true or not, some in the family certainly used it to try to extract homage for themselves. Aunt Theresa was well into her mid thirties when she married Uncle Benny. The family had been waiting for a 'proper' marriage for her but with none forthcoming and age catching up with her - in those days people married very young - they settled on Uncle Benny. Although rough around the edges he was presumed trainable.

Many in that family never relinquished their superior attitude. Some traveled abroad and received the shock of their lives when they saw themselves regarded in much the same manner as their darker skinned counterparts. This was much too upsetting.

Michael and Tiffany came over the next evening to meet Mother and Brenda. Mother had already made herself quite at home in my kitchen and the delicious aroma of pigeon peas soup greeted my arrival at home. We all sat down to dinner together. In typical Rebecca style Mother bonded quickly and completely with both Michael and Tiffany. By the end of the evening he had already shown her the scar from his wound and they were both calling her Mother.

"Son, I hope you an' Bunnyface tie de knot before me an' Brenda leave to go back home."

I realized that this was the occasion in her life that Mother had secretly been waiting for - a daughter's marriage. I'm sure over the years she had resigned herself to the fact that it might never happen.

"Certainly Mother," answered Michael. Right then we phoned the church I attended, which unfortunately was booked up but they were able to reserve the last Saturday in August at another church for us. So the date was set for August 31st; two days before Mother and Brenda were to return home and before Tiffany would start a new school year.

"Aunt Boni... can I be your bridesmaid?" asked Tiffany.

"Of course," I responded even though we had not yet given any prior thought to a format.

The following Saturday, at a little get together at my house, initially intended for Mother and Brenda to meet a few friends, everyone toasted to the upcoming wedding of myself and Michael.

I was happy to let Mother take over the planning of the wedding, which she did with great enthusiasm. Brenda, who had an international driver's license, used my car to drive Mother to different shopping centers in the city while I was at work. She didn't seem thwarted by my warnings about the slippery streets after a snowfall. Despite the cold weather they were having a marvelous time.

"Adlyn called to invite us to a sleigh ride on the Rideau canal on Wednesday," said Brenda, one afternoon when I arrived home.

"It's freezing cold out there this week," I warned.

"Who 'fraid dat?" laughed Brenda. "Ad said we just have to dress for it."

Ad as well as Madge had loaned me a lot of winter gear for Mother and Brenda. Coupled with what I had, there was enough warm clothing for both of them. I knew that Ad, who now worked several hours a week at the restaurant was beginning to feel like the proverbial little boy with all work and no play.

"Me don' know de las' time me get to sit down for a good ol' talk wid a friend. All me been doing lately is work, work, work," Ad told me the last time I passed her in the hallway at *Universal.* So if Mother and Brenda were up to a sleigh ride, then so be it.

23

Mother, Brenda and I enjoyed sitting around the dinner table and chatting most evenings. Sometimes Tiffany and Michael would join us. The stories ranged from Nanny's youth to the present. Mother finally recounted to Brenda and me the story of *The Island Queen*. She was surprised at how much we already knew.

"Who was the young man you lost on *The Island Queen* Mother?"

"Dat was Johnny St. Jules. But who tell y'all all dis?" she asked.

"Nanny," I replied. "The week before I left for Canada. And I told Brenda."

Mother shook her head. "I tell Mama I gwine tell y'all when de time right but she won' listen. I guess she tell y'all about how Brenda come too?"

Brenda and I looked with queried faces at Mother.

"What?"

"Eh?"

Mother stood up. "Let's go sit down in the living room," she said softly as she headed in that direction, leaving the used supper dishes on the table. Brenda looked anxious. I knew this had to be an important revelation - taking precedence to cleaning up after a meal.

"You have yoh chain, Brenda?" Mother asked as she took a seat on the couch. Brenda always wore a beautiful gold chain that Mother had given her on her sixteenth birthday. I remembered wondering how come I never received a gold chain on *my* sixteenth birthday, but because I'd just returned from a wonderful holiday in the country with Nanny, I decided not to complain. Fair was fair. Brenda got the chain, I got to spend the holiday with Nanny.

"It's here," answered Brenda as she fidgeted around her neck and retrieved her chain, which she showed to Mother.

"Dat chain was from yoh mother."

"My mother? I was adopted? You and Daddy adopted me?" There was a shocked look in Brenda's eyes. I held her left hand as I sat beside her on the couch.

"No," replied Mother. "Daddy is yoh father."
This story was getting stranger by the minute.

"Who my mother? ... where she is?" blurted out Brenda as she turned to face Mother.

"Yoh mother was a young woman from Trinidad," continued Mother as Brenda and I listened intently. "One morning at home I answer de doorbell and dis young girl, pretty but kind o' sickly lookin', with a baby dat seem to be jus' a few weeks old, was standin' on de steps.

'Please ma'am" she said. 'Me name is Catherine Larson. Can I come in?'

I invite her in and offer her some milk for herself and de baby. I din' know what she wanted with me but I was drawn to de little baby from de very beginnin' - she was so cute. Bunny was ten months old at de time. I went and get her from Mama Burke to let her see dis new baby. I sit down on de couch wid de two o' dem in me lap and Bunny jus' start playin' wid de little baby who look like she want to smile. It was a joy to see.

'Please ma'am' the young girl say to me. She was so polite. 'I so sorry... I never did know Denis Burke married... forgive me ma'am, but dis is Denis child.'"

You could have knocked me down with a feather when Mother said that. Poor Brenda looked like she was about to give up the ghost.

Mother continued. "At first I din' know what to do or how to t'ink. All kind o' feeling rush at me at once. I feel vex, vex, like scaldin' she down wid some hot water but when I look at de sickly looking t'ing I feel sorry for her. She tell me dat she have a big favour to ask me. She was goin' back to Trinidad soon to spend her last days at a clinic there. The doctor said she was terminally ill wid cancer and wasn't gwine make it past de month. De pregnancy prevented her from takin' treatment for de cancer. She come to ask me to keep her child and bring her up as me own. 'Please ma'am... I know you a good woman... is not me baby fault dat yoh husband cheat on you... please ma'am take her as yoh own chile.'"

I reached for the box of tissues and after pulling a few for myself passed it on to Brenda as the tears were streaming down our eyes.

"I remember Mama tellin' me that God have a plan for everybody. We don' know what it is, she say.

But one day it gwine hit you. You have to be open. You could choose it or leave it."
I was speechless. Nanny had said those exact words to me too.

"Dat same week," said Mother, "de doctor tell me dat when I had Bunny me uterus get so damage, de chance of ever having another baby was slim to none. Me belly stay big, big ... everyone believe I was pregnant again. As I look at de two children playing in me lap, I realize dis child was de answer to me prayers. And you know me belly start going down soon after dat.

'I gwine take yoh baby and bring her up as me own daughter,' I promise Catherine.
She came over and hug me, then she take her baby out me lap. 'I just want to hold her for one last time' she say to me.

'What's her name?' I ask her.
'Brenda ma'am,' she answer me. 'Dat was me mama's name.'

'You have any picture of yourself or yoh mother for her?'
'No ma'am ... but I'll send you one.'
Catherine then take a gold chain from around her neck and put it in me hand. With her eye water running down her face, she t'ank me over and over.

Mama Burke come in de room to see both me an' Catherine cryin' our eyes out.

'Dis is Denis daughter,' I tell her as I introduced Brenda, then Catherine. Mama Burke din' say nothin'. From mornin' Denis was a womanizer. She jus' take Brenda from Catherine's arms, pick up Bunny and take de two babies out of de room.

'I better leave now before she come back' said Catherine. We embraced. She felt thin and feverish. Something tell me she din' have much time left. Catherine took the *Madinina* boat home to Trinidad that afternoon. She died in less than two weeks. I never receive a picture from her. But I had dat gold chain from her, which I give you when you turn sixteen. I din' want to give you before so you go an' lose it."

Brenda fingered the precious gold chain around her neck as she bent over and kissed Mother on the cheek.

"I may not have given birth to you," said Mother. "But we are mother and daughter."
Brenda continued to sob softly as Mother gently rubbed her back.

With that disclosure a lot became clearer to me. Brenda was not related by blood to Mother, Nanny and the Bennett side of the family. But I could appreciate the mixed emotions she must be undergoing. Her birth mother had acted heroically, making sure that her baby was in the best place possible. In a way she had sacrificed her own life for her baby's. Mother certainly raised her as her own daughter. But was there a curiosity to learn more of her biological mother's side of the family?

"So my birth mother's name was Catherine Larson?" asked Brenda after she had dried her eyes, answering my unspoken question.

"Yes," answered Mother, with one arm still around Brenda. "And yoh grandmother would be Brenda Larson."

What remained unsaid at the time, was how Mother reacted to Daddy after that revelation.

Obviously the marriage survived but I suspected there were further bumps along the road.

"Did you hear the temperature today?" I asked Adlyn on the phone the day of the sleigh ride. It was minus 30 degrees and by nighttime with the wind chill factor it was sure to be much worse. I was definitely getting cold feet, especially with respect to Mother and Brenda going on the sleigh ride.

"Cha man Boni... don' be such a damn whimp!" Ad definitely didn't want any of us to back down. "All y'all have to do is put on an extra sweater."

"An extra sweater is all we need in minus 30 temperature?"

"Me carry some extras just in case," said Ad. There was no bowing out gracefully.

Brenda seemed thrilled when I told her how cold it was. I think she saw this as an adventure, like the climbing of Mt. Everest. I was secretly relieved that Mother was coming down with a slight cold and opted to decline.

Wrapped up in layers of winter gear, Brenda and I looked like the Good Year blimp in the TV commercial. Mother took pictures of us, which she humorously said she was going to keep for blackmail purposes. I passed to pick up Tiffany before we headed down to Dow's Lake, where we met Adlyn and the rest of the group.

"Scarf, tuque, anyone?" asked Ad loudly before we got on the sleigh. She had brought a bag full of extra items. One young lady with a bare head was fashionably dressed as if going to the shopping mall. She must have an inner heat, I concluded.

With Ad's strong high-pitched voice leading the group in song, we took off on the sleigh down the canal. The driver explained that for the horses not to get overheated, they had to maintain a certain constant pace. The night was cold but crisp and the decorative lights on the canal gave it an aura of festivity. We returned the waves of many people as they skated along gracefully.

"I wish I could do that," said Brenda looking wistfully at the skaters.

"I'll teach you if you wish," said Tiffany extending an offer I was sure Brenda was going to take her up on. In that respect, Brenda had not changed since we were children. She was always ready for adventure. I continued to be the 'scaredy cat'.

Back at Dow's lake we got into our cars and headed over to *The Caribbean Kitchen* for a late supper. Everyone enjoyed the sleigh ride although in some cases toes and fingers needed to be thawed out later. Madge observed that the fashionable lady did indeed use some of Ad's gear after all.

"I thought you said we were going to be on water," Brenda said to me as she dug into some stew beef with dumplings.

"So where you think we were?" I asked her. Brenda stopped eating and with eyes like two saucers she stared at me. "We were on the water?"

"Yes," I said. "We were on water that's frozen solid."

Brenda almost sputtered. "Break me neck!" she said, astonished, as the rest of us burst out laughing.

"That's the world's longest skating rink," said Tiffany, happy to be able to impart this bit of knowledge to her new auntie.

It was indeed astounding what absolute changes could occur in nature from one season to the other.

24

With major help from Mother and Brenda our wedding plans were coming along fine. I had agreed that Michael finish the basement of my house which we would use to host a small wedding reception. Having done that and also the necessary landscaping in the Spring, Michael would have as much equity in the house as I did and we would become equal partners.

Adlyn had warned me, "Is none o' me business but don' act fool-fool jus' for love girl. Mek sure unnu get a prenuptial agreement." She was pleased with this arrangement.

The Caribbean Kitchen was catering the wedding; Mother and Brenda were making the wedding cake and taking care of the flowers; Sharon had offered to do the decorations; Fleurina was making my wedding gown and that of my maid of honour and bride's maid. I had already chosen the wedding invitations and Michael and I were discussing a format both in the church and for the celebrations. Everything was moving ahead smoothly or so I thought.

After two years in university, Sharon decided to switch her major to Business with a minor in computer science. At first Ad was suspicious. "It mean she have to stay on a whole nudder year at university," she said to me. "Me no know what r--- t'ing dat pickney pullin'."

"But look at what her major is in," I urged her. I didn't know what Sharon's plans were but I felt a major in Business could be a great help not only to her but in her own father's occupation. "And everyone needs computer skills these days."

"Yoh right," admitted Ad finally as we both parted after having coffee together at *Universal's* coffee shop.

Back in the clinic, I picked up the telephone receiver on my desk to listen to any recorded messages that had come in while I was at coffee. I heard Regina's irate voice accusing me of plotting to steal both her husband and her daughter. "Well I have news for you," she concluded. "I never signed the divorce papers and I have no intention of doing so. So there!" In that I was sure she was wrong. Both Regina and Michael at different times had told me they were divorced. So she must have signed the papers. But I couldn't believe how my once best friend could become such a vicious pit bull towards me. I thought of all those times when we exchanged confidences around my kitchen table. Where was all that anger coming from?

Michael was taken completely off guard. He and Tiffany visited Regina, who'd been at home sick for a couple of weeks, at her new residence in a down town apartment. McIvor, it seemed, had jumped ship. He was no longer in the picture. While Tiffany watched TV in the living room, Regina lured Michael into the bedroom and made a surprising play for him. When he resisted, she accused him of abandoning her and slapped him squarely in the face, threatening she will never sign divorce papers.

I learned that some technicalities had been overlooked and the divorce had never been formalized. My initial instinct to go talk to Regina was strongly discouraged by Michael. So in the midst of everything, all the expenses we were undergoing, it was now necessary to hire a lawyer to untangle this mess. I think both Michael and I were beginning to feel overwhelmed.

On my arrival at home later after stopping off at Michael's, I found Brenda smiling from ear to ear. She'd been talking to Stonehead who'd informed her that the plans for opening the clinic in Grenada were moving ahead speedily. Two other physicians, currently practicing in New York were interested in joining him and a target date had been set. Brenda was thrilled. There was a new joy in her eyes these days. "He said to say hello and congrats to you," said Brenda. "He wanted to know if you'd consider joining us, but when he heard of your wedding, he realized there was no hope."

"No hope? There's never no hope," I replied still a little discouraged from the confusion Michael's divorce situation had thrown me in.

Michael and I didn't say anything about this problem to Mother and Brenda, and I kept stonewalling whenever Mother wanted us to get going with the invitations.

"It's just a small wedding, Mother," I told her. "People don't need months notice."

"Bunny please... you bein' so difficult..." Mother reprimanded me. Sometimes when I was with my mother I felt like I was nine years old again. Released from the shade of her well meaning though stunting protection and direction, like a flower gravitating towards the light, my petals had gradually unfurled. I was determined not to regress. But I knew she was having a hard time wondering why I had suddenly become so sluggish with the wedding preparations. I didn't know how much longer I could keep stalling.

Gratefully the basement-finishing project was to start the following week and Mother accepted that that should be almost through before invitations were sent out. It was no point putting an address for the reception before we were absolutely sure. For my part I was thankful for the four to six weeks time that process would buy me. Surely by then all that divorce mess would be solved.

I confided these fears in Fleurina, who was making the bridal gown as well as the one for Brenda, the maid of honour and Tiffany - the bride's maid. Not only did she give me an ear to vent but she went much, much further. She offered to hold off on starting the gowns until the beginning of July. Madge had told me that Flo usually took July and August off with her family, so I deeply appreciated her generosity and hoped it wouldn't come to that. She also invited Mother, Brenda and Tiffany to spend the upcoming long weekend with her family in Toronto. "It will give you and Michael some time to talk things over and to chill," she said. We certainly appreciated her kindness. I don't know what I would have done without that woman.

25

After a few ups but many more downs it became obvious that the basement project would not be finished to our satisfaction in time for the wedding reception.

"Why don't you rent the party hall at Southpark?" suggested Tiffany. That was an excellent idea that neither Michael nor I had thought of. As luck would have it, the hall was available and we were able to book it.

There was no argument from Mother when I told her that during my upcoming vacation, the last two weeks of June, we would get going on the invitations. We were also looking forward to some traveling during that period too - going to Montreal, Niagara Falls and Toronto.

The weather had suddenly improved. It was generally sunny with moderate temperature. Brenda went walking with Mother or jogging by herself almost every day. I couldn't pinpoint the reason but there seemed to be an extra glow about Brenda ever since Mother told her the truth about her parentage. Most days when I arrived home from work I found them in the park behind the housing complex. If at home Brenda was sure to be grooving to the swarthy music of Roberta Flack or Luther Vandross. But like a bone stuck in my throat, I worried everyday about Regina's refusal to sign the divorce papers. There had been no movement on that front up to now.

"What a sad face!" said Mason to me one morning at work and I feigned a smile. "For someone going *en vacance* in two days and getting married in two months, *tu est très desolé.*"
Mason himself was taking the month of July off. He would be gone by the time I returned from my vacation. But more significantly, he was quitting his job at the end of September to start a new life in his beloved city - San Francisco. I couldn't imagine the clinic without his presence.

"I'm dying for a coffee," I said brushing off his concerns and picking up my purse, headed quickly out of the unit away from Mason's inquisitive eyes.

After paying for my coffee, I turned towards a darkened nook in the coffee shop, where I could be alone with my own thoughts and commiserate by myself for a while. Unless someone came directly into that section, I could not be seen.

I had just entered the section, when I noticed it was already taken by someone else, whose back was towards me. It was a woman about my age. She mopped at her eyes. Weeping silently, profusely. It was Regina.

That day I saw her in the coffee shop, Regina was a shadow of her former self. She looked thin and pale.

Beneath the Surface

"Regina," I said spontaneously, placing my hand on her shoulder before I even processed in my mind that this woman was the source of all my present problems. "What's the matter?"
She looked up at me, lips quivering, her eyes swimming in tears. "Oh Boni," she said and held my hand tightly. Resting my coffee on the table, I pulled the chair next to hers and sat down. "What's the matter Reg?" I asked again.
"They got back the results," she said. "I have breast cancer and it's spreading quickly. It's already spread to the lungs. I have to start treatment tomorrow." In the face of some problems, it is surprising how some others that were previously very important, just got relegated to the back burner. I embraced her as she silently wept on my shoulder.
"I'm so sorry Reg... but you know, you can fight this." I had already swung into military mode. "You may feel sickly after the treatment tomorrow, but I'll be there with you."
Regina looked at me directly. "Boni... I've been such an arse. I've treated you so badly." She wiped more tears from her eyes, then continued. "I'm so sorry... I don't know why you're still so good to me."
"Let's start over Reg. Let's forget the past."
It was as though we were two old friends again sitting around my rickety kitchen table.

Brenda drove us all the way from Montreal to Niagara Falls. She enjoyed highway driving, she said.
"It's so easy... no turns, twists and hills like in Grenada. I can close me eyes and do this."

"Hey! Watch what you're doing," I shouted at her as she changed lanes suddenly without signaling. The driver of the car behind honked his horn angrily.

"Is not dat damn easy," said Mother. "An' please keep yoh eyes on de road before you kill all of us."

After spending an entire day at Niagara Falls Mother was in the back seat dosing now as we headed east towards Toronto. Before going to the Falls, we'd had a few enjoyable days in Montreal and were now making our way to Toronto. Flo promised to have my wedding gown ready for fitting by the time we arrived and she would take Brenda's measurements.

Brenda sang along raucously with Ajamu, the calypsonian. "I like this fellow... he's so progressive," she said, pressing the play button on the car's CD player, to repeat Ajamu's calypso. "He's not like some others who have always tried to make us feel like a pluck o' shit."

I agreed with Brenda. Even after some albums had been reissued and brushed up, those lyrics thought funny at first but which time and sensitivity should have revealed as offensive, had not been changed. I joined Brenda loudly in song as she tapped the rhythm on the dash-board.

African lady ... I love you.

"You know Boni, you should never sing to Michael," Brenda shot a mischievous glance at me.

"And why not?"

"If you want to keep him that is... but if you want to scare him off... that voice of yours... Hee! Hee! Heeeey!" she laughed as I elbowed her severely in the arm.

"Watch what y'all doin' in front dey, okay?" cautioned Mother who was just rising from sleep.

It was the first time I was meeting Fleurina's daughters, Rena, Crystal and Monir. I'd met LilChet, her son, who was the same age as Ayanna and Tiffany, at Madge and Willie's place a few times in the past. At ages nine, seven and three, the girls were enchanting and I could tell they had their father wrapped snugly around their little fingers.

It seemed that on their last visit, Mother and Brenda had already woven their way securely into their little hearts.

"Hi Mother Burke," said Monir entwining her chubby little arms around Mother as Mother leaned over to hug and kiss her. She was no doubt Mother's favorite. "I'm coming to your wedding Aunt Boni," she said to me. This child was as cute as a button and not the least bit inhibited. Rena and Crystal both looked like Fleurina and could have passed for twins.

Later that evening Jessica and her daughter Jolene dropped by. "Thanks for the wedding invitation," they said to me. "We'll definitely be there."
Fleurina and Chester had just been telling us how Jolene won the prestigious medal of distinction at university for being the best student in her section that year. "Congratulations," I said to her. "We're so proud of you."

"This prize comes with a mentorship program," said Jessica. She looked at Jolene. "So Jo had an appointment with the Dean this morning to set it up."
Jolene smiled knowingly.

"Tell them about your appointment this morning, Jo."

We all looked at Jolene, who looked hesitantly at us for a moment then began to relate what happened when she arrived at the Dean's office for a nine o' clock appointment. "To my surprise the Dean didn't know anything about it. 'I'm so sorry' he said to me. 'If I didn't have another appointment right now, I would be happy to meet with you but I'm already booked up.' I was sure I hadn't made a mistake. The Dean's secretary had set up that appointment with me over a week ago and I had carefully entered it in my agenda. I checked my agenda again as the Dean was doing likewise. 'I have to meet with a Jolene Farrow at nine o' clock,' he said and his jaw dropped when I told him *I* was Jolene Farrow. "

"I guess he wasn't expecting someone looking like you," said Brenda.

Jolene laughed. We all got the picture perfectly. "That's right," she said. "He went totally red and apologized over and over... but you're right... he wasn't expecting someone looking like me."

"My, my..." said Mother, shaking her head from side to side.

"You see," said Jessica. "Even so called informed, intelligent people have us stereotyped."

Chester looked over at Fleurina and sighed.

"That's so dangerous..." I said, half to myself.

This past week, whenever I watched the news, there was the illustration of a black guy who was wanted for a shooting at a shopping center. Together with the composite sketch of the Ainsley park rapist, which was definitely of a black male, the media in a benign way seemed to me to be projecting a negative image of black people, especially black youth. Just among my limited circles, there were so many young people with tremendous accomplishments, but somehow those positive stories always seemed to get side swiped by the negative ones. The news media is a powerful tool in society, I thought, but it was high on negativity. It could completely distort the image of a group. Was that because people clamour for bad rather than good news? I didn't have the answers.

Silently, stealthily as if by osmosis, a negative self-image could seep into one's very being from the larger community. This could be one of the many reasons some black youth seemed to have lost their way and to have given up on any lofty achievement. I was therefore impressed to see the extent to which Fleurina and Chester went to limit and censor their children's TV watching. There were no TVs in any of the bedrooms. The sole TV in the entire house was situated in a very public area, the family room, adjacent to the dinette and kitchen area. The computer, another powerful conduit for both positive and negative influences, was also in that same room and nearby in a recessed area, was Fleurina's sewing machine. The house was perfectly set up for parental monitoring of the children's activities.

I was just thinking how lucky Fleurina and Chester were, when a remark of Flo's cut into my thoughts. "It's like walking in a field of land mines," she said. Mother and Brenda were at the other corner of the room with the children. Jessica and Jolene had left.

"What did you say?" I asked.

"Yes... a child growing up today is like someone walking in a field of land mines."

Fleurina wasn't given to exaggeration, so I waited for her to clarify.

"Let me tell you what happened to LilChet a few weeks ago," she said almost in a whisper.

I looked at Flo intently. "He insisted that even when he stayed at school late for his saxophone lessons, he could take the bus home from school by himself. He claimed we were the only parents picking up a child of his age from the school."

"You guys were making him look like a sissy, eh," I chuckled.

"I guess it was embarrassing for him," continued Flo. "But one evening at home the phone rang and it was LilChet all excited and breathless. 'Mum,' he said to me, 'I'm calling you from the *McDonald's* by the corner because a guy was following me.'"

"No way!" I said.

"I instructed him to stay right there and I was coming immediately to get him," continued Flo. "When I arrived, Chet described how this guy followed him to the bus stop. He got on the same bus as Chet. He got off when Chet got off and proceeded to follow him. At that point Chet was definitely suspicious and decided to go instead to a nearby *McDonald's* and call home, instead of walking home on a fairly quiet street."

"He did the smart thing."

"Yes... thank God he did."

"Lord only knows what would have happened if this guy had gotten hold of him."

"A child was assaulted and raped in that same area that very night," said Flo softly.

I gasped. I understood clearly now what she meant by that land mines comment.

Fleurina found time to volunteer at her children's Elementary school, once a week. "I enjoy it," she said. "And I can even bring along Monir, who is now crazy about starting school."

Little Monir was talking to Mother a mile a minute while showing her something in a picture book. "But I've discovered just how ignorant some parents could be. You know how many times I've seen a teacher cussed out by a parent?"

I recalled my incident with Mrs. Howard, Tiffany's English teacher, that no doubt Fleurina had heard about. She touched my hand. "I'm talking about parents who don't give the teacher a fair chance. They just come in and start a brawl."

"That happens often?"

"It happens occasionally but that's much too frequent in my opinion. Most teachers don't deserve that."

Before I went to sleep that night, I called Michael. He was happy to know that we were having fun, that Mother and Brenda were enjoying the sights and weren't getting too much on my nerves, and that the gowns for the wedding were on their way. He was still enjoying his new job in a technology firm and Tiffany was looking forward to starting her summer vacation next week.

"And we went today to water your plants," stated Michael proudly.

"You did?"

"Your hibiscus is starting to bud."

"Now that Mother's not there fussing over it, it's decided to bud," I laughed.

"You should see the garden," said Michael teasing me. "It's suddenly looking much better."

"I think Mother and Brenda fuss over it too much. What that garden needs is some neglect," I said.

Michael chuckled. "Ad went with Tiffany today to see Regina," he said to me on a more serious note.

"Yes? How is Regina doing?"

"She's doing fairly well. She asked Tiffany to say hello to both of us."

Ever since I met Regina in the coffee shop, our relationship had taken a 360 degree turn. I'd been with her the following day during her treatment at the cancer clinic and I'd taken her home afterwards. She'd been most grateful, apologetic and compliant.

"Yes? And did she get an appointment for her next treatment yet?"

"It's scheduled for next Wednesday," answered Michael.

"I'll be back by then to see her through it... I hope it goes as well as the first one did."

"My darling...you are truly the most amazing person I've ever met."

Michael had not been impressed by Regina's show of penitence. "Now that she needs you..." he'd stopped in mid sentence. Perhaps he'd been down that road before. He also didn't think she should be included in our wedding so I decided to leave our plans as they were.

"Should let you get some sleep now honey. Will call again tomorrow night," I said as we blew our good night smooches at each other through the phone.

26

I had just flicked on the TV, which was on an American channel, to watch the evening news. As I fingered the remote just before switching to a local channel, my eyes registered someone whom the police had picked up after a high-speed chase. The cameras got a close-up shot of the suspect as he was being handcuffed. He was a tall gaunt looking individual. Something glittered in his mouth as he squirmed. I recognized him immediately. That was the guy I'd bumped into at Ainsley park. He may well be the rapist.

I felt a flow of relief. Although he had not been picked up for the Ottawa crime, I was relieved that he was now off the streets - any streets. I thought of what Fleurina had told me about that close call LilChet had experienced. For the first time I felt good about my visit to the police precinct. I had given them the information I had. Now it was up to them.

I phoned to talk to Adlyn about our visit to Montreal and Toronto. We had supper with Veronique one evening and she told us all about the time she spent in England, which is where she and Ad first met.

"Until I met Ad I use to ask meself everyday why I come to this place," said Veronique. We had heard of the awful experiences many Caribbean people experienced in the 'mother country' when they tried to rent rooms or apartments or went looking for work. Some were so bitterly disappointed that they would have returned home immediately, except that going back would have been the ultimate shame. After all, it took months of preparation and sacrifice on the part of many families. Not to mention the days of partying as part of the farewell ceremony.

Veronique told us some funny stories too. Like the time a young guy from one of the smaller islands was seen wearing a woman's coat. Someone had made him a gift of that coat before he left home and being an unfamiliar garment in the Caribbean he had no idea it was a woman's. Then when she went to meet Todd on his arrival in England "all six feet four of him sported a powder blue suit in the dead of winter." Understandably that suit was a big hit in his home island but it was totally out of place with the foggy, gray English background. She had Mother, Brenda and me in stitches. I enjoyed that humorous side of Veronique that I was seeing for the first time.

"She din tell y'all how she land in England all dress up in her Sunday frock wid hat and gloves?" asked Ad.

"No," I answered. "She said that was how you were dressed." We both cracked up.

I particularly wanted to talk about Sharon with Adlyn. I'd met her for lunch while in Toronto. She was dressed way out as usual and initially said very little, replying in monosyllables to my inquiries of herself, school etc. But then it all came out. The breakup of her parents had affected her deeply. She didn't get along with her mother and her father seemed to leave everything up to Ad, whom until recently she felt, didn't like her. She was caught between two camps, belonging to neither. No wonder she sought refuge by jumping from one relationship to the other; what Ad called her alley cat behaviour.

That invitation to go to New York with her father and stepmother last October to shop for *The Caribbean Kitchen*, changed the way she saw them. Most of all it changed the way she saw herself. She discovered that she had a talent for decorating. It's amazing how a small act could have such profound repercussions.

This next semester at university she intended to work very hard. She had decided to change her major to Business and computer science, which she was sure could be useful at her father's restaurant or in the corporate world. It was going to be difficult and she expressed some apprehension as to whether she was up to the challenge. But she was determined to try her very best. I reached across the table and took Sharon's hands in my own. Looking into her eyes, I reminded her that the only way to eat an elephant is one bite at a time and that the longest journey starts with a single step.

So I encouraged Ad to 'hang in there' with Sharon as much as possible. I believed she had been a very insecure and lonely person, who was only recently finding her legs. But she was showing signs of pursuing the right path. Copying a phrase that was being tossed around these days I said to Ad "parenting is a delayed gratification activity, my dear."

The doctors were going after Regina's tumour very aggressively so she was getting high doses of chemotherapy, which made her feel very weak and nauseous at times. Myself, Tiffany, Adlyn, Madge and even Brenda and Mother, who'd never met her before, spent quite a lot of time with her. Mother brought her containers with nutritious soups for which she was very grateful. "You need to eat properly," Mother reminded Regina. "More than ever now, yoh body need fuel to repair itself."

Brenda got her an organizer system to keep track of all her medication, noting whether they were to be taken on a full or empty stomach and the time each one was to be taken.

"Let's do something about your hair," I said to her one day, when I caught her looking at herself in the mirror wistfully.

"Yes," she answered. "I think we have experience in that department already."
We both laughed as we recalled that day last year when we fixed up my patchy hair that Adlyn had damaged with a relaxer. Actually after we had taken off most of her hair and she'd applied her make-up, Regina looked like a brand new person.

"I feel so much better already," she said as she looked at herself in the mirror.

Regina divulged a little bit about McIvor to me. Without going into any detail, she said that they both had too many problems; too much baggage which multiplied when they were together. "We weren't good for each other," admitted Regina.

"Yes?"

There was a poignant silence. I knew the person in both our minds just then was Michael.

July passed by happily. Tiffany was taking voice and piano lessons. She never got to teach Brenda how to skate as the cold, canal skating weather ceased immediately after the week of the sleigh ride. But Mother and Brenda were enjoying the parks in Ottawa, where we had many picnics. They took a tour of the Thousand Islands in the Gananoque area; they found the area around Dow's lake and the Arboretum simply awesome, especially when the tulips were blooming; they visited Parliament Hill and watched the changing of the guards and more or less participated in all the 'touristy' things in the city. They loved the Art Gallery and the By Ward market area but most of all I think they enjoyed visiting with friends and the preparations for my wedding had catapulted Mother into seventh heaven.

27

Francine interrupted her month long August vacation from work to call me at the clinic. Ever since I'd discovered her treachery towards me, with respect to the Dacota case, I kept her at arms length. I was definitely aloof and cool with her.

"Boni," she said. "I'm planning the farewell party for Mason at my mother's place next Friday. Can you come?"

"I ... I ... don't know," I stuttered.

"I thought since I'm at home I can do all the planning, gift buying etc... you guys can pay me later."

"It's a week before my wedding Francine and I'm very busy." Mason wasn't leaving until the end of September, so why was this blasted woman aggravating me with this stuff now? On the other hand it was generous of her to do all the planning, gift buying and setting up by herself.

"Please Boni, I can even pick you up at the hospital after work since I'll be in the area. You don't have to stay long. You can just drop by for a little while."

"Let me get back to you Francine," I finally said. There were two persons flitting around my desk requiring my attention.

When I mentioned Francine's call to Brenda and Mother that night at the dinner table they both encouraged me to go to Mason's party. I hadn't told them what a two-faced, hypocrite Francine was. Start talking about one thing and sooner or later Mother would have all my guts spilled out. Before I knew it I would be telling them all about that incident with the preservative. And I wanted to forget about that.

"But I have to drive Tiffany to her voice lessons on Friday," I objected. "I promised Michael to do that for him."

Michael had to go to the airport to pick up his mother, who was coming in from Barbados for the wedding that same afternoon of Mason's party.

"Big deal Boni," said Brenda, throwing her eyes up. "As if I can't do that for you."

She had a point. I couldn't think of any other excuses, especially as Michael also encouraged me to go.

"Give yourself a break honey," he said. "Go and do something different for a little while."

So after work I showered, changed and basically made myself presentable in the locker room. As arranged Francine picked me up at the front entrance of the hospital and we were now driving to her mother's home at the east end of the city.

I didn't know where on earth Francine was taking me but this place seemed to be tucked away behind God's back at the arse end of nowhere. "Your mother sure lives far," I commented as she took a left turn then a right and all I saw was cornfields.

"We're almost there," said Francine.

Finally we came to a housing complex and Francine turned into one of the houses and stopped in the driveway. There were several cars already parked on the street, so I imagined many people were ahead of us.

Her mother, a red-haired woman firmly cosseted into a green sheath, opened the front entrance to the house and Francine introduced us to each other. "Please to meet you," I said politely. Behind her I waved at a few nurses from the clinic and I spotted one lady from Ad's ward too.

"Come this way," said Francine heading up a nearby flight of stairs. I followed her up. I think her mother and the other ladies followed closely behind us.

"Surprise!" shouted a group of people in chorus as we got to the top of the stairs. I looked around for Mason, whom I imagined must have just stepped into the room. I blinked in disbelief as I saw ahead of me *my* folks - Brenda, Mother, Tiffany, Madge, Ayanna, Adlyn, even Regina - all grinning, smiling but there was no Mason. It slowly dawned on me that this was not Mason's farewell party but a shower for me jointly hosted by Adlyn and Francine.

"Don't look so terrible girl, as if you 'bout to pass out," said Adlyn coming towards me laughing. I had not closed my gaping mouth in the past few minutes.

I was truly amazed. How did Ad find the time to do this? And that Francine! I hadn't even invited her to my wedding but here she was hosting a surprise shower for me. One day Francine could be a sleazy back-stabber and the next day she could be among the most decent people in the whole wide world. I remembered Mother's recent words to me, when I tried to engage her in a conversation about Father. "Bunny, you never find anyone dat is a perfect angel or a perfect devil. Everybody have good and bad in dem and the problem is dey tightly meshed in together." How true!

For a woman of fifty-eight Winifred Doyle, Michael's mother, was very youthful in appearance. The curly ponytail that cascaded from the center of her head to the nape of her neck far from being ridiculous on her added to her semblance of youth.

She hadn't seen Tiffany since Tiffany was five years old, she said and I could tell that had been painful to her. Tiffany was certainly enjoying all the attention she was getting these days.

"I have only one child," she said to me. "So I was hoping for lots and lots of grandchildren." She looked expectantly at me.

"We'll see what happens," I answered. Michael and I had agreed that we would be open to whatever comes. I had already submitted my application for the position of clinic supervisor that Mason was vacating at the end of September. If I got it, a pregnancy any time soon would be inopportune. But I wasn't a spring chicken any more and I couldn't wait forever. While I would love to experience the joy of motherhood, did I have the fortitude that it required? Did I have that strength that oozed out of Fleurina? I decided to leave it in the best hands possible - the hands of God. "We'll just see how it goes," I said again to Winifred, hoping she understood all that that implied - that I had no intention of spending thousands of dollars in fertility clinics, harvesting eggs and going to the nth degree for a pregnancy.

Winifred and I got along superbly. Initially I think she expected someone much younger and perhaps more flamboyant. She herself wouldn't be caught dead without her makeup and false eyelashes. But we both had something very distinct in common - the love of and for a special man. She told me much about her family. She was now the only one of four siblings alive.

"I had a younger sister who died of cancer," she said, "and my two brothers drowned in Helen's Bay the following month. One went to help the other that was in trouble and they both lost their lives. I couldn't take it", she said. "In less than three months my sister and two brothers were all gone. I left after that and I haven't been back to Trinidad since."

"What about your parents?" I asked.

"My mother passed away while we were still young. As the eldest child, you can say I brought up my brothers and sister."

"And your father?" I prodded.

"He provided for us," said Winifred. "We had a roof over our heads and food on the table... but that was it..." Winifred shook her head. I could tell there was much unsaid.

It was obviously a period of great sadness in her life and I didn't want her to recall that now. I thought I'd change the subject.

"Did Michael tell you that we're planning to take a belated vacation/honeymoon in Grenada and Barbados next year?"

"Oh yes," said Winifred, the sadness leaving her eyes. "And Tiffany's so happy, she can hardly wait."

"It's going to be next summer, during Tiffany's vacation."

Fleurina had driven up to Ottawa to visit her sister Madge and to bring the finished dresses. My own strapless gown fit me like a glove. It was gorgeous. Brenda was completely in love with hers. We were both impressed by Flo's superb workmanship. A slight change had to be made to Tiffany's. So before Fleurina returned to Toronto, Brenda drove Mother, Tiffany and Winifred over to Madge's home to pick up Tiffany's gown.

I was at work when Brenda called me with an odd ramble. "Are you coming home straight after work?" she asked me.

"I think so... unless I stop off at Michael's," I answered.

"Winifred and Tiffany are over here," said Brenda softly. "Michael's coming over after work."

"Yes?"

There was a strange tinge to Brenda's voice as she asked again "Boni could you please come straight home?"

"What's going on? Something wrong? What's the matter Brenda?"

"Nothing's wrong... everything's fine... but just come straight home... okay?"

"Okay," I said. I knew I wasn't going to get anything more out of Brenda.

Before I could put the key to the keyhole, the door of the townhouse was swung open by Tiffany.

"Hi Tiffany."

"Grandma, Mother, Aunt Boni's here," shouted Tiffany excitedly.

Brenda came towards me smiling. "I'm glad you came home right away," she said.

"What's going on guys?" There was a cloud of mystery hanging in the air. I wondered whether another shower or pre-nuptial surprise was on its way.

"Let's wait until Michael gets here," said Winifred.

"So she's in the conspiracy too," I said to myself. "Oh well," I mumbled as I approached the refrigerator for a cold drink. I noticed the table had been set for supper for six.

"Daddy's here," shouted Tiffany, who'd been standing guard at the front door. "Hi Daddy," she said, kissing him as she opened the door.

"What's going on guys?"

"Both of us are in the dark about what's going on," I said to him as we lightly embraced eac h other.

"Come," said his mother as taking him by the hand she led him into the living room. She seemed a bit emotional. She sat next to Brenda on the same couch where only a few months ago Brenda had found out about her parentage.

"I don' know where to begin," said Winifred holding hands with both Brenda and Michael as they sat on either side of her on the couch.

"We found out today that Winifred is my aunt," said Brenda.

"Brenda is my sister's daughter."

"Eh?" said Michael. I'd told him that Brenda and I were half sisters. He knew that Mother was not her birth mother.

"What?" I asked loudly, recalling almost simultaneously Winifred telling me that her sister had died of cancer. "What was your sister's name?"

"Her name was Catherine Larson," said Winifred. "And our mother was Brenda Larson."

"Good God!" I blurted out as I also recalled that picture of Winifred with a younger sister Michael had shown me, when Tiffany and I had visited him in Montreal. The faces in the photograph had seemed so familiar. Now I understood why. "This is a marvel. What are the odds of something like this happening?"

"Hi cous!" Michael said to Brenda, as he reached over his mother and smacked Brenda playfully on the cheek.

I wanted to know all the details. "How did y'all find this out?" I asked.

"We were talking and joking around about ugly pictures," said Brenda.

"And Grandma decided to show us her passport picture," said Tiffany.

"We were all jokin' at it, when I take another look at de name on de passport," added Mother. "It say Winifred Larson Doyle."

"So Mother said to Winifred 'Yoh name Larson? You have the same name as Brenda's mother.'"

"When they told me Brenda's mother name was Catherine Larson, I couldn't believe it." Winifred was still wiping tears from her eyes.

"I tell Winifred how Brenda's mother died of cancer shortly after she bring her baby to me."

"By then I was convinced... I din' need no more proof... and Catherine called her baby Brenda, which was our mother's name."

After she'd gotten pregnant Catherine had been sent away and Winifred and her brothers had not been allowed to contact her. But Winifred had heard the rumour that Catherine went to Grenada to stay with her boyfriend. "I never knew when the baby was born or what it was," continued Winifred. "One day my brother came home with the news that Catherine very sick at Meadow Hill clinic. I went to see her that same day but she din' know me... she was out of it by then. She died that night. No one knew anything 'bout a baby."

There was a long silence in the room. We all felt that a miracle had occurred in our midst. I thought to myself if such good could come from the union of Michael and me, then surely that was a sign that we were meant to be.

28

Behind Brenda, my maid of honour, dressed in a splendid off-the-shoulder, pale yellow gown and Tiffany, my bridesmaid, in a deeper shade of yellow, I was escorted down the isle by Mother, looking more beautiful than I'd ever seen her before, in an elegant suit of beige lace. The hair dresser and make-up artist, who'd come to the house that morning had worked miracles on our hair and face, succeeding in making us all look stunning.

Mother and I had promised each other that we wouldn't cry and mess up all that expensive eye makeup. But when I saw my groom waiting for me at the end of the isle all dressed in military regalia, with his mother Winifred and one of her husband's brothers, who'd come for the occasion, I had to try hard to stem the flow.

Here comes the bride ... all dressed in white began the wedding march as all the guests in the church stood up.

Sharon had done a beautiful job of decorating the church and Tiffany had disclosed that the reception hall was even more exquisite. The flowers and the wedding cake were a gift from Mother and Brenda while Sharon had done all the decorations and I had not been allowed to go peak.

Tiffany surprised almost everyone with her stunning rendition of *Ave Maria* and later the *Panis Angelicus*. Not many present had heard her perform before and were taken aback. The sermon by the priest was to the point and moving.

Then came the wedding vows, which we had written ourselves. Michael went first. "I Michael Jerome Doyle, swear to you, Boniface Burke, that you are and always will be the love of my life, my soul mate, my queen. You are my sustenance, the waters that quench my thirst. I have been blessed to find you, a gem of purest ray, serene; a flower beautiful and sweet. Today I solemnly pledge that I will give you the best of whom I am at all times. I promise to love, respect and cherish you forever. So help me God."

I think I was holding my waters very well until this point. The damn was about to burst forth. I blinked back the tears. It took everything in me to stop them. I closed my eyes, cleared my throat, took a breath and began. "I Boniface Burke do solemnly swear that I will love you, Michael Jerome Doyle, with all my heart, for the rest of my natural life on this earth. Nothing will come between us or sever the bond of my love for you. As long as God gives me life, whatever hurdles may confront us, together we will overcome them. I will be there to comfort, cherish and to love you. In my heart you will find your nest; in my arms, your home. I do solemnly swear." I think Michael was the one trying to hold back the tears now.

As I walked back down the isle, this time on the arms of my husband, I blew kisses at Mother in the front seat with a young gentleman, whom I did not recognize but who nevertheless looked vaguely familiar. I nodded at Jessica, Curt, Joshua and Jolene behind them and at Winifred and Veronique with her children on the opposite side. Michael did likewise as cameras flashed in our faces.

Before going to the reception hall, which was at the Southpark complex, we headed over with the bridal party to the Arboretum and Dow's lake to take pictures. The guests went ahead to the patio in front of the reception hall where they were served hors d'oeuvres and drinks until the bridal party arrived.

I was so excited with all the goings on that I hadn't given any more thought to the gentleman I'd seen with Mother at the church. Several of Michael's relatives had flown in for the wedding. Most of them I was meeting for the first time. But this guy was next to Mother on the bride's side.

Now as I entered the hall through an archway of flowers, so beautiful, so artistic, thinking what a beautiful job Sharon had done, the gentleman by Mother's side smiled at me. "Stonehead!" I shouted, as it suddenly hit me that that was my cousin Stonehead whom I hadn't seen in seventeen years. Completely forgetting decorum and cameras we rushed to each other.

He had arrived in Ottawa the evening before. Mother and Brenda had called him months ago and invited him to be the surprise guest at the wedding. "I wanted to see how long it was going to take you to recognize me," he said as he touched his receding hairline. "I haven't changed that much."

"Same Stonehead," I laughed.

I introduced him to Michael. "I think I know you already," Michael told him. "I've heard so much about you."

"And I'm sure it was all good stuff you heard," said Stonehead jokingly.

"Of course," replied Michael.

The bridal party greeted all the guests as they entered the hall. Fleurina, Chester, their son LilChet and daughters Rena, Crystal and Monir wished us blessings along with Madge, Willie and Ayanna. Herbie, Adlyn and Sharon, as well as Mason and a couple of folks from *Universal* also offered us good wishes. Mason was busy doing a video of the wedding, which was his gift to us. I met several of Michael's relatives on his father's side for the first time.

The Caribbean Kitchen served a meal that was delicious and luscious. Ad and Herbie had put out their very best for the occasion. The master of ceremonies, who was one of Michael's cousins, read cablegrams that we had received from well-wishers and relatives who couldn't be there. Among them was one from Lucille and Patty's two daughters in California. More surprising was one from Todd, wishing us all the best. Veronique later gave me the good news that Todd had finally signed a teaching contract in Alberta.

Some of the speeches were funny, others were poignant, but all were full of love and good wishes for Michael and me. One of the speeches that resonated in the hearts of everyone was Winifred's. She told the guests that this wedding was a match made in heaven.

"How do I know that?" she asked as she looked around at everyone. "I received a sign from heaven," she said. "I had a sister who'd passed away many years ago. I won't go into the circumstances of her death, but she left behind a child, with whom I was unable to establish any contact." Everyone was listening intently. Winifred smiled. "Just this past week," she continued. "I found my niece, my sister's daughter and she's right here now." Winifred walked towards Brenda at the head table and they hugged each other. "This beautiful young lady, sister of the bride, is my niece," she said as everyone applauded thunderously. I saw the surprised look on Stonehead's face. I knew Brenda had already told him that Mother was not her birth mother but I'm sure he was as surprised as everyone else to find out that her mother was actually Michael's aunt.

Next came the dancing - the part I loved the most. Michael and I danced together to our favorite tune *Love Conquers Everything* after which we separated to dance with close family members. Michael went for his mother and I chose Stonehead. Finally all the guests were invited to shake a leg. Some smart ladies slipped into more comfortable shoes at this time and so were not in the least bit encumbered. The D.J. did a tremendous job in catering to the tastes of the young people as well as the more senior, which was no easy task. I saw Rena and Crystal boogying down with Ayanna and Tiffany.

Every time I looked at Stonehead he seemed to be dancing with Brenda. But it was the way they held each other, the way they looked at each other, that made me wonder whether something was brewing between those two. I decided long ago that there's nothing like going straight to the fountain if you want a drink.

"Tell me the truth," I said to Brenda as I danced over to their area on the dance floor. "What exactly is going on here?"

Brenda laughed loudly and whispered something into Stonehead's ear. He laughed too and drew her more closely to him as he nodded at me.

"Let's just say," said Brenda leaning over to me. "Fair exchange is no robbery."

"What you saying?" Even though she'd pretty much told me I was still flabbergasted.

"Cousin for cousin," said Brenda laughing raucously as she danced away in Stonehead's arms.

Michael and I checked into the honeymoon suite of a downtown hotel in Ottawa that night. It had been a most enjoyable day. Everything had gone as planned - even better than we could have imagined it. Now as I looked at my husband I couldn't help but appreciate just how beautifully made he was; dark chocolate coloring, flat stomach, muscled chest and shoulders. A quiver of awareness flowed through my being. Something in his eyes told me that he liked what he was looking at too. He had that flushed look, that special look; that look that left no doubt in my mind that to him I was number one.

ISBN 141208943-3